Rolling On

Also by Jamie Sumner

Deep Water
Maid for It
One Kid's Trash
Roll with It
The Summer of June
Time to Roll
Tune It Out

Rolling On

JAMIE SUMNER

 ATHENEUM BOOKS FOR YOUNG READERS
New York   London   Toronto   Sydney   New Delhi

ATHENEUM BOOKS FOR YOUNG READERS
An imprint of Simon & Schuster Children's Publishing Division
1230 Avenue of the Americas, New York, New York 10020
This book is a work of fiction. Any references to historical events, real people, or real places are used fictitiously. Other names, characters, places, and events are products of the author's imagination, and any resemblance to actual events or places or persons, living or dead, is entirely coincidental.
Text © 2024 by Jamie Sumner
Jacket illustration © 2024 by Amy Marie Stadelmann
Jacket design by Karyn Lee
All rights reserved, including the right of reproduction in whole or in part in any form.
ATHENEUM BOOKS FOR YOUNG READERS is a registered trademark of Simon & Schuster, LLC. Atheneum logo is a trademark of Simon & Schuster, LLC.
Simon & Schuster: Celebrating 100 Years of Publishing in 2024
For information about special discounts for bulk purchases, please contact Simon & Schuster Special Sales at 1-866-506-1949 or business@simonandschuster.com.
The Simon & Schuster Speakers Bureau can bring authors to your live event. For more information or to book an event, contact the Simon & Schuster Speakers Bureau at 1-866-248-3049 or visit our website at www.simonspeakers.com.
Interior design by Jacquelynne Hudson-Underwood
The text for this book was set in Adobe Garamond Pro.
Manufactured in the United States of America
0824 BVG

10 9 8 7 6 5 4 3 2
Library of Congress Cataloging-in-Publication Data
Names: Sumner, Jamie, author.
Title: Rolling on / Jamie Sumner.
Description: First edition. | New York : Atheneum Books for Young Readers, 2024. | Audience: Ages 10 up. | Summary: "Thirteen-year-old Ellie finds herself faced with first love and learning to let go as her friendship with best friend Bert starts to turn into something more, and her beloved grandfather loses his battle with Alzheimer's disease"—Provided by publisher.
Identifiers: LCCN 2023030624 | ISBN 9781665947848 (hardcover) | ISBN 9781665947862 (ebook)
Subjects: CYAC: First loves—Fiction. | Family life—Fiction. | People with disabilities—Fiction. | Alzheimer's disease—Fiction.
Classification: LCC PZ7.1.S8545 Rp 2024 | DDC [Fic]—dc23
LC record available at https://lccn.loc.gov/2023030624

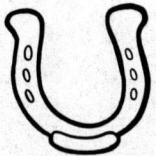

For my Jonas
whose heart is ≥ to Bert's

Rolling On

1
Welcome Home!

You can't unsmell a smell. Once it's there, it's there for life. And every bus smells the same—sickly sweet gas and smoke-choky exhaust. It sends me right back to elementary school and waiting for the wheelchair lift to take its fine time cranking down so I could roll on up. The bus depot in McAlester is no different, but this time I'm sucking it in like sweet, sweet Christmas pine, because Bert is coming home.

"You got the sign?"

"No, Ellie, I left it in the trailer," Coralee deadpans.

"You're hilarious." I glance over at her, bundled in a silver puffer coat and white earmuffs. I see no sign. "Wait . . . you do have it, right?"

"It's in the Caddy. Chill." She jerks a mittened thumb back toward where Susie, Coralee's step-grandma, waits in the car.

"Well, go get it!"

"You go get it!" She shoves me, so I pivot and roll toward the car. Susie passes me the sign through the window, which was already down despite the subzero temps, because she's back on the Camels. She says she'll quit again for Lent. We'll see.

"Here, darlin'. Birds got at the corner a bit, but the rest is fine." Susie winks. She says the trailer full of cockatoos is more hazardous to her health than the smokes.

A bus screeches to a halt behind me and the doors are already whooshing open by the time I get back to Coralee, who shakes her head.

"Always be prepared. That's what I say. You almost missed the big welcome home."

"Shut it and help me hold up this sign."

She takes one end and I take the bird-nibbled corner and raise it high. I clock Bert as he's jogging down the steps with a duffel bag larger than he is slung over his shoulder. He looks . . . different. His dark hair, usually so neat and combed, is a big mess of whirls and spikes, and is he taller? Maybe it's just the sweatpants. Wait, Bert is in sweatpants? Where are the ironed jeans? What is *happening*?

"Girl, higher!" Coralee hip-checks my shoulder and lifts the sign so he can get a clear view.

One thing you've got to know about Bert. He's never in a hurry. So when he eventually nudges his way around the other tired passengers hunting for their family and friends on this cold January morning, I am jumping up and down in my seat to keep the blood flowing to my extremities. I would like to take my toes back home with me, thank you very much. He spots us on the sidewalk, eyes the sign, and tilts his head. No grin. No wave. Just a nod and then a slow jog over to us.

"Who's Robert?" he asks.

"What?" I say. I'm trying to wriggle my toes, make sure they're intact. Also, I'm busy studying him. It's like my memory has laid a picture of Bert side by side with this new one and I'm trying to spot the differences.

He points to the sign. "It says 'Welcome home, Robert.'"

"In glitter," Coralee adds with a grin. That girl would do anything for a tube full of glitter glue.

"It's your name, Bert," I explain. He blinks at me like I'm the one not in on the joke.

"I know that."

"Jeez, man." Coralee punches him on the shoulder. Between his navy fleece and her mittened hand, I doubt he even feels it. "We were trying to be funny."

He looks at me. "You never call me Robert."

He's only been gone two weeks, but with the two weeks before that when I went home to Nashville to visit my dad and his wife, Meg, and my half brothers, this is the longest I've ever gone without seeing him.

I clear my throat. "Well, things change," I say.

He nods at both of us. Then, finally, he smiles—a real Bert smile that crinkles the corners of his eyes, and something in me flutters, like the fin of a fish brushing past you in the murky dark of a lake. It's not bad, just . . . weird. I pretend it isn't there, like you do with all the things you can't see underwater.

"Come on," Coralee says, making Bert carry his own sign. "Your parents'll think you never came home from this fancy-pants science camp of yours. We promised we'd drop you off at the Food & Co. so they could see you right away."

"I think they've already scheduled you for a shift," I joke, but not really, because Bert's parents' grocery store is a family business and everyone pitches in when they can. Now that all his siblings have gone back home after the holidays, they need all the help they can get.

"It wasn't science camp," Bert says as we make our way through the frosty morning light. "It was the Kentucky Young Environmentalists Consortium, and we were required to complete rigorous academic courses as well as individual capstone projects in order to receive the certificate of achievement at the end."

Coralee opens the back door for me and asks him while I'm transferring in, "And did you complete this capstone-y thing and get your certificate, Roberto?"

"I did." He points to my chair. At my nod, he folds it up and loads it along with his duffel in the trunk. Then he hops in the back with me, and his cheeks and the tip of his nose are pink and the collar of his jacket is tucked inside his sweatshirt, and for one crazy second I want to reach over and straighten it. *What is wrong with me?*

Bert talks for the entire thirty-two-minute drive from McAlester to Eufaula. But I do not hear one word about the Kentucky Young Environmentalists Consortium or his project or the dorm rooms at the boarding school where it was held. Instead, I watch the light sparkling on the frosted grass along the highway and I count the tar-covered lines on the concrete road that are taking us home and I *do not* think about the fish-swishy feeling I got when Bert, one of my best friends, smiled at me.

2

Food for Thought

Food & Co. is hopping at ten a.m. when we cruise through the front doors. It's the "Holidaze Extravaganza"—the annual sale when everything red and green, from plastic sandwich bags to pickled pigs' feet, is half-price. I once asked Bert if anyone bought the green pigs' feet at any price and the answer was yes, yes they do. And also, ewww.

I grab a handful of spearmint candies from the barrel by the cash register because Mr. Akers says no one eats those anyway and follow Bert and Coralee toward the meat department, where Mrs. Akers is waiting with an apron and a hug.

"I swear you've grown!" she says, draping the apron over his head while also trying to pat down his hair.

He ducks away. "The average height of the males in our family is six foot one, and this is a prime growth year for most adolescents. The probability is high."

She wipes an invisible smudge from his cheek. "I missed you."

"Aww." Coralee nudges him.

"All right, sappy stuff over." Mrs. Akers hands him a hairnet. "I need someone else to slice the pastrami so I can get back to the bookkeeping."

"I've got it, Mom. You go," Bert says, tugging on the hairnet and plastic gloves like he's about to perform surgery. That's Bert. Home five seconds and already down to business.

"I'm off, then," she says with a little wave, but then she leans toward me. "Can I get a sneak peek at whatever welcome-home treats you've made for this little reunion first?"

I blush. She's right, of course. I did bake. It's something I thought Bert would especially appreciate, except now I'm embarrassed. I'm not sure why.

I motion for Coralee to pass me the grocery bag I made her haul in from Susie's car. Then I unload paper dessert plates with little candy canes on them and red forks that, yes, I bought on super sale from Food & Co. yesterday. I was trying to be festive, but now it seems silly. Still, I give the green tablecloth that I borrowed from Mema's Christmas linens a shake. I spread it over the sample table by the deli counter and place the Tupperware in the center. Everybody gathers around while I unsnap the lid.

Inside are twelve perfect chocolate marshmallow-stuffed cupcakes topped with chocolate ganache and a little white squiggle of icing. I was going for old-school Hostess vibes. You'd never guess it, but Bert has the biggest sweet tooth of all of us. When his eyes light up, my cheeks go red, again.

Coralee doesn't wait for an invitation. She grabs the one with the most icing, skips the plates and forks altogether, and dances over to the counter, where she props an elbow next to the green pigs' feet and digs in.

"Pretty sure you just got chocolate up your nose," I tell her. Mrs. Akers also takes one, puts it on a plate as God intended, and then heads to the back office.

"Don't come at me, El," Coralee says through a mouthful of crumbs. "Susie's gone sugar-free post-Christmas."

"She quit sugar and picked up smoking again? That's a recipe for success." I'm only half paying attention to what she's saying, because I'm too busy watching Bert to see what he thinks of my creation. Out of the corner of my eye, I see him take a bite. He chews way too slowly.

Coralee rolls her eyes. "You're tellin' me. Dane says

she's trying to kill him. I say this is her midlife crisis a few decades late."

I turn to Bert. "Well?" He lifts the cupcake up under the fluorescent lights, and I hold my breath. He's never shy with his opinions, and he would never lie to me about my cooking, or anything else. It's one of the reasons I trust him. It also annoys the crap out of me.

I throw up my hands. "Forget it!"

He sets it back down and gives me the "Bert look"— head tilted, mouth quirked up on one side, like he's either studying me or having an intense conversation in his own head.

"It's pretty much perfect."

"Pretty much?" I cross my arms. Coralee leans back to watch.

He pokes the filling in the middle. "Could use a touch more marshmallow cream."

I roll my eyes. "You *would* say that. There's not enough sugar in the world for you."

He nods, granting my point. Good to know some things about Bert will never change. Bonus: his honest opinion has chased the fish-swishy feeling far, far away.

Coralee claps once, like she's the director of one of her beauty pageants. "All right, people. I hate to cut this reunion short, but the clock is ticking. The old Caddy's temperamental in the cold, and so is Susie—she won't wait forever. School starts back Monday. Any pertinent info we need to swap to get prepared? Ellie—Mr. Hutchinson, Hutch, er, your stepdad, is he still driving us?"

I nod. It's been half a year since Mom married my gym teacher, but Coralee and Bert still don't know what to call him when he's not at school.

"Bert, you got an alarm set on your phone to remind Mr. Hutchinson, Hutch"—she throws up her hands—"whatever, that we have to be there fifteen minutes early on the first day?" She may fumble over his name, but we all know Hutch is not a morning person and needs all the help he can get. Coralee and I aren't any better, and Mom teaches at the high school and has to leave even earlier, so she's no help. It's up to Bert and Bert alone.

He nods, and then we all sigh over the little bit less sleep we'll get. As if we need that first morning back to be even rougher than it already is.

Coralee rallies first. "All right, people." She grabs two more cupcakes and holds them up like trophies. "Here's to the grand finale of middle school! Let's go out with a bang!"

I sigh again, this time on the inside. Coralee is my other best friend, and I would tell her *almost* anything. But I will never tell her that I'm not over-the-moon excited about high school. I don't want to start over in a new building with new aides and therapists. I don't want to lose Hutch as my gym teacher. I don't want to learn a new floor plan or wait and see which teachers remember to rearrange their rooms to make them wheelchair-accessible.

I might be the only eighth grader in the world to say this, but I don't want to leave. Is it so bad to wish everything would just stay the same?

3
You Win Some, You Lose Some

Dear Sally of Sally's Baking Addiction,

 I made your Cream-Filled Chocolate Cupcakes for a friend—a best friend, actually. They were amazing, of course. I did as you suggested and "bloomed" the cocoa in hot coffee, and they were so much more chocolatey! I also made the marshmallow meringue, because I am a pro at meringue after this summer's beauty pageant Baked Alaska fire extravaganza. That's a story for another day.

 But I have a confession: my intentions

were not entirely selfless in making this boatload of sweetness as a welcome-home gift. The real reason I made the cupcakes was because I need to be the best. In your monthly baking challenge, everyone was posting pictures of their own version of the cupcakes, and I can never resist a competition. I've got the annual pie bake-off coming this spring in my town. I need the practice. I need to make sure I can measure up against other bakers. I need to test my skills. I've got a friend who's really, really good at science and I want to be really, really good at something, too.

    I'm pretty sure my science-y friend thinks this private school where the camp was is better than our school now. It's all he talks about. He probably thinks the kids there are better than us, too. But I bet none of those kids can bake like I can. They know science, but they don't know baking science! They don't know that salt can make something sweeter and that brownies and banana bread and cheesecake are better the next day and that smells are the quickest triggers of memories.

You know what? I'm not one bit sorry that I had other motives for making these cupcakes, because they reminded me how awesome baking can be and how awesome I am for rocking it. Thank you for that.

All my best,
Ellie

"I cannot believe this new early-morning meeting is why the entire eighth grade has to lose *fifteen more minutes* of sleep at the beginning of every month," Coralee whines while we sit in the gym, waiting for . . . whatever this is.

Outside, the sky is still dark but turning pale gray at the edges. It's the opposite of Grandpa's magic hour, when everything glows rosy and wonderful just before dark. This is the slap of cold morning, and nobody's happy about it. Bert yawns next to me. Ms. Wilson, the assistant principal, sees him and does the same. It sets off a chain reaction among the faculty, and now everybody's yawning. I can practically see Hutch's molars from here.

Finally, our principal, Mrs. Rutherford, stands up and moves to center court. She might be old, but with her height and the size of those black no-nonsense pumps, I bet she could play a mean game of basketball in her day. She looks right at home.

"Ladies and gentlemen, I hope you all had a wonderful and restful winter break." To her right, Mr. Barlow, one of the science teachers, yawns. "Thank you for gathering here early on this lovely January morning."

"As if we had a choice," Coralee whispers not-so-quietly. Mrs. Rutherford shoots her a warning look.

"As eighth graders and pillars of leadership in this school, we look to you to set a good example for the younger students."

From my front-row spot in the bleachers, I hear more whispers behind me and turn to see who else thinks this meeting is a waste of time. It's Sierra and her friends, but they're not looking at Mrs. Rutherford. They're looking at Bert. A signal flare goes off in my brain. I am always on the lookout for danger when it comes to Bert. After a rough start in sixth grade, Sierra and I have finally gotten to a good place—not friends, but at least in a truce. Bert, however, with his factoids and satchel and neatly creased pants, has always been an easy target. She better not be making fun of him. I watch her and her friends study him. They aren't laughing in a mean way. They're *giggling*? It's like a happy-to-see-him, we-just-spotted-a-TikTok-star giggle. What. Is. Happening?

I look back to Bert, who is rubbing his eyes. The satchel is firmly in place across his shoulder. But his hair is uncombed again, like it was at the bus station. His pants are not creased. He looks younger than his usual put-together self, which makes him seem like an actual thirteen-year-old for once instead of a thirty-year-old man trapped in a child's body. Another giggle rings out softly from behind me. They like it. Clearly.

So it's not my imagination, and I'm not the only one who's noticed the change in Bert. This is not good. Bert cannot handle loads of attention. Like Batman, he prefers to do his thing and stay in the shadows. I want to ask Coralee about it, but Mrs. Rutherford has moved forward as she's been talking and now she's only a few feet away.

". . . let these final two quarters help clarify your goals and priorities."

In the pause that follows, the gym begins to rustle like an orchestra warming up as everyone gathers their backpacks and breakfasts and jackets. But Mrs. Rutherford isn't done.

"In conclusion," she says, not any louder than before, but in a tone that makes everyone go still, "you may think you have all the time in the world, but high school is just around the corner. Make the most of these final days as you follow your passions and perhaps discover new ones. Thank you. You are dismissed."

Sierra and her crew thump down the bleacher stairs, and she gives one last look at Bert, who is busy zipping up his jacket and doesn't notice. She sees me see her and waves. I give her a little wave back, because despite the fact that the way she's looking at him makes me want to shove her, I can at least be civil. Coralee frowns and stuffs half a Pop-Tart in her mouth, because she won't even pretend to like Sierra. Now I'm beginning to wish I didn't have to, either.

After mostly everyone has filed out, I follow Coralee and Bert toward first period. There is still a whole day left. I am already exhausted. Coralee is outlining the passions she plans to pursue in order of priority—"One: singing, two: dancing, three: acting, four: cat-taming." That last one's new. Bert is talking, mostly to himself, about some wind farm he learned about at his Kentucky consortium. Mrs. Rutherford must have given one doozy of a speech that got everyone pumped for high school, but I have *no idea* what she said. I was too distracted by Bert and the girls who now love him. I stop by my locker and gently rest my forehead on my knees. What is wrong with me?

Three classes pass in a whirl of cautionary speeches from teachers. Apparently, they all got the memo that this half of eighth grade will determine our entire future. The only class I'm doing well in is English. The rest I skate by right in the middle—not low enough to set Mom on alert and not high enough to give the teachers any ideas about honors and extra-credit opportunities. Unpopular opinion: I am happy to be mediocre here. School isn't my jam. Baking is my jam, pun intended.

Bert and Coralee are already at our table at lunch by the time I wheel over with my tray of chili cheese tots. Coralee pops the lid on a wilted salad and groans.

"Susie is really and truly going to be the end of me," she says, and steals a tot. Then she grabs Bert's paper bag and dumps the contents out on the table like a Christmas stocking.

"Fake meat and pretzels and orange slices." Coralee pokes each item as she speaks. "Bert, the cockatoos eat better than this. I was counting on you for some discounted ham rolls at least."

Bert pulls out a fork. "I'm experimenting with vegetarianism."

"Since when?" I ask.

"The director of the consortium, Mr. Blackburn, is a big proponent of plant-forward meals," he explains.

"Ohhh, well, if the director says it's the thing to do, then I guess I had better give up my fried-bologna-and-mustard sandwiches," Coralee says while trying to steal another one of my tots.

"You should definitely do that anyway," I say, shoving her hand and turning back to Bert. "What does Maya think about this new vegetarian thing? It's not like there's a whole lot of meat-free places to go for *date night* around here."

It's a low blow. We became friends with Maya at the beauty pageant this summer, which she entered so she could practice her onstage skills for the Scripps National Spelling Bee. She has a brain just as big as Bert's, which is why they hit it off, I guess. And I *like* Maya, so I don't know why I'm teasing him about her.

Bert clears his throat. "We, uh, haven't talked much since I left for Kentucky. She said she needed to focus on the Bee."

Huh. So he and Maya aren't a thing anymore. The fish swishes its tail again, totally uninvited.

"You win some, you lose some, kiddo," Coralee says, patting his hand and then slowly pulling his pretzels toward her.

Bert shrugs. "It's okay. And you're right," he says to me. "Though Cracker Barrel does serve a decent vegetable plate, she probably wouldn't have enjoyed the local vegetarian options. Did I tell you about the dining hall at Brighton Academy? That's the boarding school where the consortium was held." *Yes, Bert, you might have mentioned it two or three hundred times,* I say in my head. "More than two-thirds of their selections are plant-based and locally grown. There's a garden on the property, and the students are in charge of tending it. Their lentil loaf was given an A-plus rating by the US Department of Agriculture."

Bert's face lights up as he describes lentils and sustainably sourced kale and how eco-farming is a crucial step in fighting the climate crisis. He steals my spoon and knife to fence off a portion of the table to create a diagram that demonstrates exactly where the gardens were located on campus. There is even a greenhouse, where they grow fresh herbs all year round. My baking self is intrigued at the potential for fresh ingredients anytime I'd want them. My fish-swishing self is most definitely not amped about how happy he looks about the joys of another place far away from here.

This is what's different about Bert. It's not the hair or the clothes or the fact that he's in an epic growth spurt. It's that he's excited about something. I may not have heard much from Mrs. Rutherford's speech this morning, but I did hear the bit about finding your passion, and Bert has obviously found his. Confidence comes when you find the thing you love and follow it. I would know. This consortium has clearly helped Bert find his. I should probably just be grateful that the camp thing only lasted two weeks and he's back now. But still.

I steal back my spoon to scoop up the rest of my chili, which is cold and gloopy now. It ruins his garden, but he doesn't notice. As he talks, his eyes crinkle just the way they did when he tried my cupcake. Maybe more.

I shake off my first-day stress in gym. It's my favorite class of all time, because (1) there's no homework other than what I specifically request from Hutch, like free-weight cross-body wheelchair work, and (2) you don't have to talk, you just have to *move*.

Today is roller derby day. Two points to my new stepdad for knowing I would need to get all my feels out on the track. Last fall we all had to sign a waiver to even be able to do this. It basically said we wouldn't sue the school if we broke a nose, kneecap, or any other body part while participating in the derby because the derby is no joke. It goes like this: Two teams. One jammer on each team, who scores a point with every opposing player they lap. The jammer wears a helmet with a star. The rest of the team is responsible for protecting the jammer and blocking everyone and anyone who might want to slow the jammer down, because the jammer is always the fastest one on the team.

I strap on my hot-pink helmet with the black star, because I am the jammer, of course. I'm already rolling into position while the other girls are struggling to buckle their skates. Coralee rolls up next to me, our breath steaming in the cold winter air.

She taps my elbow pad with hers and nods. She is my best blocker. We do not smile. This is serious business.

"All right!" Hutch shouts from the starting line. "Highest total number of laps at the end of three races wins." He puts his whistle between his lips, then takes it out again. My hands itch to grab my wheels. "And remember, this is a no-contact game, people. Keep it friendly." It is not my imagination that he looks right at me. I grin, and the corner of his mouth lifts. He readies the whistle again and backs off the track. My fingers tingle with anticipation as I hold them over my wheels like a pianist over a keyboard. Time to make the magic happen.

At the sharp tweet, the blockers take the lead and I follow my team, weaving in and out of the opposing players as Coralee makes a path for me. Most of the skaters are so wobbly that they fall when they feel me close. Amateurs. The wind whips my hair and cuts straight through my sweatshirt, but I don't feel the cold, only the freedom.

By the third race, most of the girls on the opposite team don't even try to get in my way. Their legs shake with the effort to balance on the rough track. But I've spent a lifetime preparing for this. My body absorbs every bump and turn without a flinch. By the time Hutch blows the whistle signaling the end, I don't have to count to know I've won. I pop a wheelie and coast over to Coralee, who has thrown herself on the ground near a pile of similarly splayed teammates. She is too out of breath to talk, but she holds a fist straight up in the air and I bump it.

Maybe the rest of eighth grade won't be so bad after all.

4
On the Mend

At four o'clock in the afternoon, the sky isn't much brighter than it was at morning assembly. The gray is a solid sheet that stretches across the open plain as far as you can see. Bert and Coralee and I huddle in a tight circle to shield ourselves from the Oklahoma wind and wait for Hutch to pull the van around to the front of the school.

That old familiar bus smell greets me with a puff as the last of the students line up to load. Sierra grins at Bert just before she steps in. He blinks at her. Cole and Jackson catch her looking at him, and my shoulders tighten. They are the two worst human beings ever to have graced the fine city of Eufaula. At first, Jackson just looks confused, but Cole narrows his weaselly eyes and breaks line to walk over. It's a slow walk full of bad thoughts and future bad deeds. I can feel it. Coralee sees it, too, and we squeeze tighter on either side of Bert. We are not just a huddle; we are a shield. I wish gym weren't split up into guys and girls. I would give anything to meet those two in a roller derby race.

"Hey, pals." Cole slaps one hand on Bert's shoulder and the other on the back of my chair. I shove it off. No one touches my chair without my permission. He keeps a grip on Bert, who blinks at him in much the same way he blinked at Sierra. "Everybody have a nice break?" His smile could cut glass.

"Yeah, *pal*, we sure did," Coralee drawls. "Your mama give you a DNA kit for Christmas so you could finally figure out if you're human or reptile?"

He smiles wider, then barks a laugh, making me jump. "You're one to talk, girlie. You're as cold-blooded as they come."

Coralee pulls back her hand in a fist. My heart scampers and disappears into a pit of fear. I couldn't move if I tried. But Bert does. He places a firm hand on Cole's arm. Cole jerks his head away from Coralee and toward Bert.

"Oh, you're a tough guy? Is that why all the girls are looking at you now?"

The bus driver honks his horn. Jackson puts one foot on the first step, but Cole doesn't budge. We need them both gone, *now*. I roll back an inch, just enough so the whole weight of my wheel lands on Cole's baby toe. He squeals and dances backward, but not before pulling Bert's satchel off his shoulder as he goes.

"Not much of a man if you carry a purse, huh?" He hurls the worn-out insult at the same time as the bag, then limps off to the bus.

"It's a satchel!" Coralee shouts, chasing him and kicking the bus doors just as they close.

Bert looks toward the bushes where his bag lies next to the flagpole. I roll over, pick it up, and bring it back. The shoulder strap is torn completely off one side. He holds it up by the broken end and examines it. Every ounce of excitement from lunch is gone. His face is a mask, and I can't bear it.

I take the satchel from him and curl it into my lap. "I'll have Mema fix it. She can fix anything."

"Don't worry about it." It's Bert's voice, but it's not. It's all hollowed out. He reaches for the satchel, but I hug it tighter.

"No, really. I promised her and Grandpa I'd go over there anyway after my first day back."

His arm falls. "Okay," he says as Coralee runs over,

huffing white clouds of steaming anger into the air.

"We'll get him back," she says just as Hutch arrives, popping the van door for me.

"No," Bert snaps, the blankness of his voice gone. "I don't want a fight."

Coralee throws up her hands. "You never want a fight!"

"Let it go, Coralee," I say softly, moving toward the van so they'll follow and leave each other alone. We've had enough conflict for one day.

After Hutch takes Bert and then Coralee home, he swings back around and drops me off at Autumn Leaves, the retirement community where Mema and Grandpa moved when Grandpa's Alzheimer's got to be too much for them to manage alone. They are the reason I am here in Eufaula in the first place. Mom and I would never have moved all the way from Nashville if it weren't for them. I have them to thank for my friendship with Coralee and Bert. And Mom met Hutch because he was my gym teacher at Lakeview Middle. Mema and Grandpa gave us a brand-new life.

"You sure you don't want me to come in?" Hutch asks after I am settled in my chair on the sidewalk. He sounds like a gentleman, but really he knows Mema will dote on him like the son-in-law she never had before. Which is true. Even though my dad has started to make an effort this past year, he still can't reach the celebrity status of Hutch. In Mema's eyes, he's the one who made our family whole. And he is *such* a sucker for the attention.

"Thank you for the ride, but no. Go home. Maybe run some laps around the garden. I saw you chasing kickballs today while I was stretching on the mats. You could use the cardio."

He takes off his cap and points it at me through the open window. "Meet me in the canning shed after dinner tonight and we'll box it out with the bag. See who needs the cardio then."

"Fiiiiine." I pretend to be put out, but I love the punching bag. Nothing relieves tension better than an explosion of chalk dust after a really solid hit.

Once Hutch pulls away, it takes me a minute to orient myself. All the condos look the same—peach brick with tan shutters and an intercom and buzzer by every door—but the streets in Autumn Leaves are designated by level of care. Mema and Grandpa started out on Crabapple, and that was okay. Even though they weren't with us in the trailer, they still got to live their lives—garden, cook, fish. Then they moved to Maple, which was a little smaller and came with a daily visit from a home nurse. Now they live on Birch Street. You don't want to be on

Birch. It's where the nurses rotate twelve-hour shifts all day long, so you have round-the-clock care. It's the last step before the move up to the big house, the long, squatty building at the front entrance, which is basically a straight-up nursing home. Forget patios and kitchenettes and a view of the pond. It's hospital beds and meal trays and antiseptic spray for the rest of time. I cruise down Birch until I see number 344 in shiny chrome on the doorpost.

The door swings open before I even have a chance to hit the buzzer. It's Anvi, my favorite one of Grandpa's nurses. She smiles, her dark hair pulled into a no-nonsense bun, but her lips are bright pink. I always want to ask her where she got the lip gloss, but then get too shy.

"Hey, Eldorado. What's shakin'?" she asks. For the longest time, I thought she was calling me some kind of burrito. I didn't know an Eldorado was a car until Anvi explained it to me. She said it's because she digs my wheels. She's big on nicknames.

"Marianne-gelo, you got a visitor!" she calls. Mema's "Marianne-gelo" because the quilts she stitches are works of art. Grandpa is simply "the Whale," because of Jonah in the Bible story. All her nicknames are at least as long as the originals.

Mema shoos her with a dish towel. "Go on, now. Take

your break. I think between me and Ellie, we can hold down the fort for a bit."

I roll back to let Anvi pass, and she grabs her giant purple puffer coat and heads out into the night. I've never thought to ask where she goes on her breaks. Probably to the big house. If I were her, I'd hightail it out of here, maybe to Braum's to get myself a Black Forest sundae with extra cherries.

After Anvi leaves, Mema pulls me into a hug, her long gray braid tickling my nose and her rose lotion taking me back to when we all lived in the trailer together. She'd rub it on my feet at night on the back porch while the bug zapper sizzled mosquitoes into oblivion. I squeeze her tighter. I hate Birch Street.

"Been waiting for you all day, baby girl," Mema says, and steps back so I can follow her out of the cold and into the warm, narrow hallway. There's a smell coming from the kitchen that is so familiar it sets my mouth watering, but I can't place it. She sees me trying to work it out.

"Three guesses."

"Sugar cookies?"

"Nope."

"Snickerdoodles?"

She shakes her head again as Grandpa tiptoes up behind her with his finger to his lips.

"Ummm, pecan rolls?" I guess, just as Grandpa tweaks her on the elbow, making her jump.

"I swear you're going to give me a heart attack, old man!" She slaps him on the arm.

"I've been messin' with you for over fifty years, woman. What makes you think I'm going to stop now?" He winks at me. I wink back.

"Come on, Ellie, let's go hide in the kitchen where it's safe." She steers Grandpa back toward the living room, where every light is blazing because it's already dark outside, and night is Grandpa's hardest time.

"Peanut brittle! I can't believe I didn't get that!" I cry when I see the caramel brittle studded with roasted nuts hardening on pans lined with tinfoil. They are shiny with butter, just the way I like them.

"Don't ever let anyone tell you dessert's only a holiday treat." She takes a piece, breaks it in half, and hands a piece to me. "Life needs sweetness running all the way through."

"You might want to tell Susie that. I think Coralee's going to float away on a sea of iceberg lettuce."

Mema chuckles and I take a bite. The crunch is perfect.

"So, young lady, how was the first day back at school?"

And there it is. The ultimate question. I let the brittle

melt on my tongue to buy some time. But the stuff is too dang good, and it's gone before I can come up with a cheerier answer.

While she makes cider on the stove, I tell Mema about the early-morning assembly and how everyone is sooooooo excited to get middle school over with and move on to high school. Then I tell her about Bert's consortium and his new vegetarian zest for life. She only stops me once.

"What the devil is satan?"

"No, Mema, seitan, *say*-tan." She stares at me. I shrug. "I guess it's some kind of meat substitute . . . like tofu."

"I tried tofurkey last year in the cafeteria up at the big house." She jerks her head toward the nursing home that sits like a white block on the black checkerboard of the parking lot. "Tasted like nothing—like absolutely nothing." She shakes her head like it's a crying shame.

I finish with the incident by the buses after school and unhook Bert's satchel from the back of my wheelchair. She wipes the last sticky bits of brittle from her fingers and takes it from me to inspect. It looks even worse in the glow of the kitchen. The busted end is frayed, and there's a big gaping hole in the corner where the seam split.

"Hmmm, might have to trim a new edge here, but

should be fixable. That's if I have a sturdy enough thread to get through this canvas. Follow me, let's check."

I know she can do it. Mema can fix anything. And I know I can tell her anything. We might not be on the back porch on our rocking couch, but we can still talk it out. A tiny flicker of guilt slows my roll as I follow her down the hall toward the bedroom. I told her everything *except* the bit about the new fish-swishy feeling when I'm around Bert. There's no point. She can fix the bag, but she can't fix that.

"Jonah! We're going in the back. I got some stitching to do!" she hollers toward the living room, where Grandpa sits in his favorite chair that we made sure to haul over from the trailer. It is the ugliest thing you've ever seen—cracked brown pleather. The handle on the side is so splintered you risk a digit every time you want to pop the footrest.

"I've got to turn this thing inside out if I'm going to do it right," she says once I'm cozied up on the bed and she's riffling through her box of spools. "Empty it for me, if it's not already."

It's not heavy, so I don't expect much to come out, and I'm right. When I tip it over the flowery comforter, a few of Bert's favorite Bic fine-point pens, a graphing calculator, and a bunch of papers slide onto the bed.

I pass the bag over to Mema and pull the contents into a little pile by my side. I'm straightening the papers, because Bert is *very* particular about wrinkles in his homework, when the heading on one of them catches my eye. I wasn't snooping. I swear.

Merit Scholarship Application to Brighton Academy: Student Information Form.

Say what? My heart triple-beats. This must be old—an extra copy of something he had to fill out for the winter consortium. I scan the rest of the page. There is a place to fill in any awards and special recognition. And a section for "Scholarship Category of Interest," with little check boxes where you have to choose between Academics, Leadership, Performing Arts, Athletics, and Global Engagement. And below all that at the very, very bottom is a due date of March of this year. *This year.* As in the future that is way past Bert's winter camp.

I slam the paper facedown on the bed and burrow my head into a pillow that smells like roses. But it doesn't help. Actually, it is *suffocating*. I can't breathe! I sit up and throw my legs over the edge of the bed. I'm angling for my wheelchair, but I'm too shaky to stand and pull it over to me. The hum of the sewing machine slows to a purr as Mema lets her foot off the pedal. She knows something's up. I curl onto my side away from her. I can't look at her right now. I can't look at anything. The nugget of hope that Mema can make things better crumbles to dust.

Bert's *leaving*. He's leaving Lakeview Middle for this big important school . . . in Kentucky! Bert is going to live in Kentucky and I will be here, and that is like nine hours away or more. I don't even know how many hours it is, because I didn't need to know until ten seconds ago. And it probably doesn't even matter because he won't want me to visit anyway because he will be too busy growing basil in the greenhouse and eating seitan in the dining hall that probably looks exactly like the one in Hogwarts and he will forget all about me and I will still be here, in a trailer in the middle of Oklahoma! I throw my hands over my face and groan.

"What in the ever-loving world has gotten into you?" Mema pokes me in the shoulder.

"I cannot believe I made him squiggle cupcakes!"

"What? Who?"

"Bert! I made him welcome-home cupcakes and they took me *hours*, because I had to make the marshmallow meringue *and* a ganache. I bloomed the cocoa!"

"You better start filling in the blanks or I'm calling Anvi to check your vitals."

I flip over so I'm facing her, even though I don't want to.

"I just found a form in Bert's bag for a scholarship to the school he went to over break. It's for *next year*. He wants to leave me . . . us . . . me and Coralee. He wants to go to high school all the way in Kentucky."

"Oh boy." Mema lays the satchel on the bed. Its shoulder strap has been reattached. Good as new. That's just wonderful. I push it off the bed.

"What a traitor." She locks eyes with me, quirks one brow. "Should we shred the bag?"

I sit up. "Yes."

She holds eye contact until I break first. "Fine. No. But I *am* tearing that application to pieces!"

"He can probably get a new one."

"That's not helping!"

"Would tearing up the form help?"

I punch the bedspread. It is too soft and totally unsatisfying. "Stop being reasonable!"

Mema scoots her chair closer. "Honey, it's just a sheet of paper. You don't know what it means. And you're not going to know until you talk to Bert."

I shake my head. "Uh-uh. Not doing it. I don't want to talk to him about this. I'm not even supposed to know about it. He'll figure out I snooped and found out his secret. I didn't think we kept secrets, but I guess I was wrong." An image of Bert's eye-crinkling smile as he finished the last of my cupcake at the counter of Food & Co. swoops in totally uninvited. "I was wrong about a lot of things." So much for using my baking to prove I'm just as good as his camp friends. I huff. "He has his secret. Now I have mine."

"There's a saying: 'Least said, soonest mended,'" Mema explains.

"What's that supposed to mean?"

"It means that you should get over what's bothering you and move on."

I open my mouth to retaliate, but Mema's not done. "*But* I think that's hogwash. I think mending only happens once you turn everything inside out so you can see all the holes."

I throw my arms over my face. "I don't want to see this hole!"

"Ellie," Mema says in her that's-enough-of-that voice, "you talk to that boy about what's bothering you. Bert is one of your best friends. And I will not have a granddaughter who says, 'I'm fine,' when she is clearly not. That's not how you were raised. You speak your mind." She pulls my arms away from my face. "Do you hear me?"

"I hear you."

"But are you going to *listen?*"

Mema's used to getting her way. I am not one to argue with her, usually. But I open my mouth to do just that when a giant crash makes us both jump.

I'm in my chair and out the door before Mema can shake the stiffness out of her knees and stand. Bonus to wheels: they are always faster than feet. I take the corner like it's the Indy 500, but as soon as I get a glimpse of the kitchen, I grab my brakes and freeze.

Grandpa is standing by the stove waving around a sheet pan. The peanut brittle it once held is all over the floor—along with the contents of every single cabinet and drawer. Measuring cups lie in a sticky puddle of spilled cider. The gallon-size bags have been dumped out and mixed with the snack-size ones. My first thought is, *It'll take Mema forever to sort those out.* My second is, *Is that* blood *dripping from Grandpa's arm?*

"Jonah, listen to me," Mema says from behind me. She's out of breath from hurrying. I'm out of breath from fear. "You need to put that pan down and come on into the living room. It's almost suppertime."

"Don't mother me, woman!" he shouts, and I flinch. Mema doesn't. She's used to it. "Where's my awl?"

"We left your awl and all your other woodworking supplies back at the trailer." She sounds calm, but when she puts her hands on my shoulders to pull me back, they shake.

"Why the hell would we do that?" he yells. His eyes are white and wide and mean. My hands tighten on my wheels, but with a rush of guilt, I force myself to let go. This is *Grandpa*. I don't need to be afraid of him. But I still can't look at him. I drop my eyes to the blood drip, drip, dripping from his arm onto the scattered peanut brittle instead.

"We did that when we moved here."

"Moved where?" Grandpa turns in a frantic circle.

"We're at Autumn Leaves, hon," Mema explains, and does not add, *Don't you remember?*, because the doctor said that only makes him more agitated. "We had to leave your tools behind because there's not enough space here." *And because things like saws and awls are dangerous.* I flinch as he starts waving the sheet pan around again.

When he gets distracted by the pile of sugar packets he knocked off the counter, Mema whispers, "Hit the button, Ellie." There's one in every room. This one's on the wall right next to the light switch. I reach for the button with a shaky hand. It will page the nurse.

Grandpa sees me press it. It lights up red like Rudolph's nose and will stay that way until someone comes. I shrink back from his glare, my heart thumping in my ears, and bump into Mema.

"I need my awl if I'm going to finish Ellie's cupcake mailbox." He takes a step forward.

"Grandpa, you finished it!" I gulp. "And I love it. We put it right at the end of the driveway a couple of years ago. Don't you remember?" The words escape before I can reel them back.

His eyes flash with anger, anger at *me*. "I don't—You can't put up what's not finished! You're not making sense!" he shouts, and lifts the pan over his head. I squeeze my eyes shut tight.

The door bangs open, and Mema whips me back just as the pan slams to the ground. Another nurse, not Anvi, runs in with heavy steps, and takes Grandpa by his bleeding arm. He twists and tries to wrench it away. He's shouting and kicking at all the stuff scattered on the floor and my face is wet because I guess I started crying, but I don't remember when.

And then it's over, like a summer storm. Grandpa goes limp and hangs his head and lets the nurse lead him to his favorite chair. "Well, how'd that happen?" he asks in a small voice as the nurse begins to wipe his arm with alcohol swabs and wrap it in gauze.

Behind me, Mema mumbles something, but I can't

understand what it is until she repeats it a couple more times.

"He wasn't going to hurt us." She says it over and over, "He wasn't going to hurt us," until Mom and Hutch get there twenty minutes later.

5

Small Comforts

Dear Jocelyn of Grandbaby Cakes,

   I am writing to thank you for your chicken-fried steak recipe. It came at exactly the right time. The cornstarch made the buttermilk batter extra crispy like you promised. We didn't have cube steak, so I beat a few thin cutlets with a rolling pin to make them tender. Walloping them like a punching bag did me good. I needed something to do with my hands.

   You wrote in the recipe that fried meat is comforting and addictive. I agree. It settles down in your belly like a warm blanket and makes you feel solid when nothing else does. Even though no one in my family had much of an appetite when we finally got around to eating it, the few bites we did manage were as soul-nourishing as you said they'd be. We needed a boost. You see, we had a rough night last night—well, my grandpa did, which means we all did. My mema says what happens to one of us affects the bunch, because that's how families work. I guess she's right. She usually is.

So thank you for creating this recipe. My mema also says any food can be comfort food if it's given by the right person at the right time. I wish I could always be the right person at the right time. For now, though, this did the trick.

Your fellow Southerner,

Ellie

When I wake up, the sun is pinstriping the floor in light, and overhead the squirrels are making a racket scrabbling across the tin roof. Mom must have let me sleep in, even though it's only the second day of school. I squint at my phone. It's nine o'clock and I have seventeen missed calls and thirty-two texts from Coralee that start with u better be srsly injured bc if not i will do it myself and eventually dwindle to u ok?????.

Susie must have taken her and Bert to school. Which means Mom and Hutch are home, too. Which means last night was not a dream and Grandpa really did cut his arm and throw a baking sheet and forget where he lived. I rub my eyes and burrow down farther in the bed.

Mema wouldn't come home with us last night, even though we begged. By the time we left, her nose was raw from crying, but her mouth was set. She wasn't going to leave him. I wish I could go back in time and have them both here. I wish they'd never left to live at Autumn Leaves.

"Hey, baby," Mom says from somewhere over my head. I pull down the covers. She's still in her blue bathrobe, which is too thin for winter, and her hair is smushed in the back. Hutch hovers behind her in the doorway with a giant mug of coffee in his hand. It's the one that reads LORD, GIVE ME STRENGTH, with a mouse lifting a barbell. It's Mema's, and it makes my heart hurt.

"That for me?" I push myself up into a sitting position. Mom fluffs my pillow. When she's anxious, she fusses.

"Nice try," Hutch says, his voice gravelly from sleep

or tiredness or both. "If I'm going to teach the last four classes, I need every sip."

"Battleball day, yeah?"

He groans.

"Sucks for you, man." This is what *I* do when I'm anxious—I joke.

"You're coming too." He points his mug at me. "If I don't deliver you to Coralee soon, she's going to file a missing person report."

Mom cups my face in her hands. "You don't have to, you know. Yesterday was a lot. We can stay here, play Scrabble, finish the Christmas fudge. It'll be nice, just us girls!" she says, lifting her voice at the end like she isn't all busted up inside.

I shake my head. "You've got class, too. Those high schoolers aren't going to teach themselves *The Odyssey*. Besides, I have to give Bert his satchel back now that Mema fixed it. I don't think he knows how to walk straight without it." I paste on a smile. Faking happiness must be genetic. Mema would pitch a fit if she saw us. We're not holding anything up to the light today. We are full-on burying our holes of hurt in heaps of good cheer.

Mom hugs me too long and won't leave until I swear I will text her immediately if I need to come home. "You are my priority, baby girl. School comes second.

Always." I pinky promise to text and then, much too soon, I am sitting in the van watching Lake Eufaula pass underneath me as we cross the bridge into town and off to school.

When I finally roll into school at lunch, Coralee doesn't even let me lock my wheels at the table before she grabs my shoulders and leans in so close her nose is inches from mine. Her blond hair falls in a frizzy curtain around us both and blocks out the rest of the room long enough for her to whisper, "*What* in the *world* happened to you?" I shake my head with a *not now* look and she backs off with a *this is not over* look of her own. Coralee and I can have entire conversations without uttering a word. It is both awesome and terrible.

As Bert unpacks a small container of hummus and an environmentally-friendly snack bag full of snap peas, I pass him his newly repaired satchel. Before he looks at it, he looks at me.

"Are you okay?" he asks, his brown eyes locking on mine. I breathe in and the air scratches my throat.

"Yeah. I'm good." Again with the fake happy.

He nods and passes me a snap pea dipped in hummus. He believes me, because we don't lie to each other. And then he carefully wipes his hands, lifts up the satchel, and studies it from top to bottom. "Amazing. Your grandmother is a wizard."

I wish. If she were, she could fix a whole lot more than bags. I crunch on the snap pea and let the salty hummus fill my mouth so I don't have to reply. I do not mention Grandpa or the scholarship application. In fact, for all of lunch I don't talk at all. Coralee fills in the silence with a story about her grandpa Dane's tooth getting chipped on one of Susie's healthified granola bars. I guess it's one of the few original teeth he has left, and he's taking it personally.

As she talks, I keep sneaking looks at Bert's satchel. A corner of the application pokes out of the open flap. I could grab it right now and wave it in front of his face and make him talk to me. But then I'd have to tell him why I care so much, and my shoulders sag at the thought, because I am so tired—from not sleeping, but also from worrying about Bert, who I never had to worry about like this before. He was always just there and the same and would always be there in the future, exactly the same. And I'm tired from worrying about Grandpa, who is definitely not the same. I never know which version of him I'm going to get. I'm thirteen. I'm not supposed to be this *tired*.

"Give her some space, Francis, jeez!" Coralee swats at the cockatoo hopping from one foot to the other just over my head, where he perches on Coralee's bedframe.

"Are birds even allowed to have meat?" I ask as Francis inches closer to where I've unwrapped the chicken-fried steak sandwich I couldn't manage to eat at lunch.

Coralee steals half of it. "Well, he's eaten tinfoil out of the trash before, so I bet he could manage, but we aren't giving him the chance." She scoots onto the floor and pulls out a glittery pink Caboodle from under her bed.

"My secret stash," she says, and winks at me when I lean over at the sound of the lid popping open. "Here, go fetch." She throws a handful of Goldfish crackers into the farthest corner of her room, and Francis flutters to the ground and attacks them with ecstasy. She unwraps a Milky Way and breaks it in two, offering part to me as a trade for the sandwich.

"My half's smaller," I say, then shove the whole thing in my mouth. I'm grateful for the sugar. I'm about to fall asleep right here in a pile of her fuzzy purple pillows.

"Beggars can't be choosers," she says through a mouthful of chicken-fried steak.

I point at her with my Milky Way wrapper. "Look who's talking."

"Girls?" Susie calls through the door.

Coralee's eyes go wide in panic. She kicks the Caboodle under her bed and tosses the rest of the Milky Way at me just as the door creaks open.

"Do I smell choco—? Oh, Ellie. Hi, love. I didn't know you were here." Susie's sweatshirt with the puff-paint snowman on it looks a little looser, so I guess the diet must be working. But she's watching this Milky Way like it is the last Milky Way on earth.

"It's Ellie's, Sus. I swear!" Coralee crosses her heart and gives Susie the baby deer eyes.

"Well," she says, her eyes still on the candy, "just make sure you take it all with you when you leave. I don't want Dane to be tempted."

Dane. Right.

Just as she's opening the door to leave and I think we're in the clear, a bright orange furry flash streaks through the crack and dives straight for Francis, where he's still happily pecking at his Goldfish in the corner.

Coralee scoops Francis up at the last second, and the ball of fur crashes into a plastic milk crate. Beauty pageant trophies clatter to the ground. "Dang it, Bunny, get out of here!" she shouts. "Susie, you know my room's off-limits!"

Susie throws her hands up and backs out. "And you know I can't control that cat. You want her gone, you catch her."

"Bunny is . . . a cat?" I sit up to get a better look. Sure enough, a bright orange tabby with the biggest green eyes I have ever seen sits on her haunches in the corner. She twitches her whiskers in my direction, licks one paw, and then delicately rubs one ear. "Aww, she's cute!"

Coralee retreats to the bed with Francis, who squawks once at Bunny and flies to the headboard for higher ground.

"Don't be fooled. She's as mean as they come. She left bite marks on Dane's cane. Daisy's so scared of her, she won't come out of her dog crate. Also, we had nine cockatoos, but I'm pretty sure there're only eight now." Francis squeaks above my head. Bunny watches him.

"The amount of time she can go without blinking is unsettling," I say.

"Tell me about it."

"Why didn't you say you got a cat?"

"It was a belated Christmas present from my dear old mom, who dropped by with her boyfriend, Roy. I got Bunny. Susie got a set of fuzzy dice for the Cadillac. Dane got a package of Hanes undershirts. And *she* left with a check for five hundred dollars for rent." Coralee rolls her eyes. "Merry Christmas to all."

She grabs a tennis ball and lobs it at Bunny, who hisses like a demon and runs from the room. "But my news isn't what we're here to talk about. We are here to talk about you and where you were this morning, young lady."

She settles in next to me on the bed, and the familiar feeling of her arm against mine is enough to make me almost cry. I swallow the tears and finally begin to talk about what I've started to think of as the "Peanut Brittle Incident."

When I'm done and my mouth is dry from too much talking and too many Milky Ways, Coralee lays her head on my shoulder and asks, "So now the people at Autumn Leaves think your grandpa should move into the big house?"

"Yeah, but Mema says no way. She put her foot down. Like for real. She was in Keds and it was on carpet, so it didn't make much noise, but it got her point across. The nurses backed off. But we still have to meet with his doctor next week."

"What does your mom think?"

"She's doing that thing she always does. She says she wants whatever's best, but she won't tell me what she thinks that is."

"And what do *you* think?"

I've only been to the big house a few times. The first was when we took a tour on move-in day, and I wasn't really paying attention because Grandpa already had a condo address with a tree-named street far enough away from there that I could pretend it didn't exist. And then, last May, we went for a Mother's Day brunch. The greeters pinned wilting carnations on Mema's and Mom's pastel dresses and the waiters dished up eggs that smelled like baby vomit in a formal dining room that looked like it belonged on a cruise ship. Nobody was fooled.

"I don't want him to go," I whisper. Coralee takes down my bun and scratches my head. She says there's no point in growing my hair out if I always put it up, but I've had short hair my whole life. When I was little, it was easier. There were too many emergency visits to the hospital when long hair would get in the way of the feeding and oxygen tubes. So we cut it off. Mom and I both. Even after I was more stable and not getting sick all the time, I kept it short out of habit. Then we moved here, and I was shaken out of *all* my habits. The hair seemed like the next step. I'm still getting used to it.

"It'll be okay," she says, like she knows. But she doesn't. Nobody does. We never should have let them move in the first place. *I* never should have let them move. Mom talks all the time about the importance of advocating for my needs—fighting to get the equal treatment I deserve in school and in the big wide world, too. I should have done that for Grandpa. I should have fought harder to keep him home. The guilt rises with a sickly sweet taste of sugar at the back of my throat, so I change the subject and tell her about Bert's application.

"That sneaky geek!" she shouts, and I smirk, because her getting mad makes me feel a little better. "He's going to leave us for greener pastures—literally! Isn't Kentucky like miles and miles of horse farms and grass?"

"Pretty much," I say, thinking back to when we drove through from Nashville, when it was one state over, not *three*.

"Well, this is unacceptable."

I throw my hands up. "What are we supposed to do about it?"

"I'll tell you what." She stands on the bed with her hands on her hips and her head almost touching the popcorn ceiling. Francis lands on her shoulder. She looks like a pirate. "We tell him he *cannot* go. And if he won't listen, we find a way to stop him. He may think he can run off to join the geniuses, but he is underestimating us, because we are *evil* geniuses!"

"Yes!" I yell, because I've been screaming inside my head since yesterday and it feels good to let it out.

Coralee jumps up and down, shaking the bed so that I bounce and Francis flutters to the ground.

"We will not let some rich school steal Bert away!"

"Yes!" I cheer again.

"And we will prove to *Roberto* that we are the *best* thing that ever happened to him!"

"Yesssssssss!" I clap, and she falls next to me just as Bunny darts in again and takes a giant leap at Francis, who flies into the bookshelf, knocking over a stack of magazines. They were hiding a stash of Cheetos, which now rain down onto the floor and bring Susie running.

She's more mad about the Cheetos than the cat.

I look at Coralee. "Busted." We burst into giggles.

I am halfway down the path back to my trailer and feeling better than I have in days before I realize that Coralee never said *how* we were going to do any of this.

6
A Way with Words

If you're going to go to all the trouble of mounting a TV in every corner of a waiting room, why not put on something good? Nobody wants to watch CNN or golf. Nobody. Give me a cooking show. Or *The Avengers*. Anything that will distract me from the fact that we are waiting for a nurse to call Grandpa's name so that some neurologist who sees him once a month can decide his fate. At least back when I had to see my own brain doctor, they had a fish tank.

Mom won't stop tucking her hair behind her ears. Mema holds one of her jumbo crossword books, but I haven't seen her pencil move. Grandpa sits with his hands folded between his knees, staring at his shiny shoes. They are his church shoes, even though they don't get out to go to church anymore. He polishes them himself with an old handkerchief and a tin of oily goo. The leather glows a warm brown like the best homemade caramel. Mema wears a navy pantsuit. I guess she didn't want to show up for a fight in a dress.

The door to the exam rooms opens and we all look up.

"Jonah Cowan?" a nurse in polka-dot scrubs barks. I don't like her tone, but Mom grabs my hand, so I decide to let it pass. When Grandpa doesn't react fast enough, the nurse calls again. She's obviously in a hurry, despite making *us* wait for forty-five minutes. Mema nudges him and he stands. I can't tell if he didn't hear her, didn't remember his own name, or just didn't want to go. That's the thing about Alzheimer's—you can never tell.

The nurse doesn't look at us after the first glance. I frown at her back. A woman like that shouldn't wear happy pastel polka dots unless she means it.

She leads us to an office that is different from the one we've been in before. We have to rearrange the chairs so that I can squeeze in my wheelchair. Once Mema and Grandpa are seated in front of the giant desk and Mom and I are crammed in behind them, the nurse leaves us with "The doctor will be in shortly," and shuts the door. Yeah, I've heard that before. It'll be another forty-five minutes, minimum. That's how these things go. It's like the security line in the airport. They block each turn so you can't see how far you still have left. They know if you did, you'd revolt.

"Well, this is cheery," I say to the backs of my grandparents' heads.

"Easy, Ellie." Mom's voice is too soft for the fighting mood I need her in.

"No, I mean it. This is a hospital. They make billions of dollars. Couldn't they splurge on a little wall-to-wall carpeting? Or maybe a futon in the corner and some glow-in-the-dark stars for the ceiling? Something to spruce this place up?"

Grandpa chuckles and Mema smiles, but Mom sighs.

"I *said* that's enough, Ellie." Her voice is tight, but strong. Good. That's the voice the doctor needs to hear.

With my job done, I zip my lips and study the walls. There's no TV. But there *is* a painting of rolling green fields against a blue sky. It looks like Nashville. It looks like Kentucky. I think of Bert. My stomach knots tighter than it already was. At least I convinced Coralee to wait to confront him until we had a solid plan, which we still don't have. It's been a week—a week closer to when his application is due.

There's a short rap on the door, and I shake my head

to scatter the thought just as Dr. Hirschman, Grandpa's neurologist, strides into the room. *One problem at a time, Ellie.*

He pumps some hand sanitizer from a dispenser on the wall and then shakes Mema's and Grandpa's hands. Mom and I get a nod.

"Alice, Ellie, nice of you to join us today."

Is it? I think, but stay quiet. I want to hear what he has to say first before I tell him how he's wrong.

"So," he says, opening the file he had tucked under his arm. "It seems there was an incident and one of the health-care workers had to get involved. As you all know, my first concern is everyone's safety." Grandpa picks at the bandage on his arm. The doctor steeples his too-long, too-smooth fingers. How's a doctor this young, with hands like that, going to take care of my grandpa? He wrangled horses and worked at the air force base and fished in the sun. The brown spots on his skin were *earned*.

Mema hunts for a tissue in her purse. Mom begins to rub a tiny circle at her temple. It's what she used to do at all my appointments. A knot of fear as hard as an avocado pit settles in my stomach.

"He was never going to hurt me," Mema says, her voice wobbly like Jell-O. I elbow Mom because it's killing me not to say anything, but she can't speak, or won't.

"Mrs. Cowan—" Dr. Hirschman begins. It's the first plop of rain in a speech that's sure to turn into a downpour. My heartbeat thumps in my ears. "We need to talk about next steps—about moving Mr. Cowan to the main nursing facility so he can receive round-the-clock medical care."

I look to Grandpa. He seems shrunken. His neck pokes out from a collared shirt that looks like it's been swapped for one two sizes too big. Why is everybody talking about him like he's not here?

I ignore the avocado pit of fear and summon all that righteous anger a good advocate needs and open my mouth. I'm done being quiet. "Nope." I shake my head. I roll an inch forward. It's all the wiggle room I've got in this tiny space.

"Ellie—" Mom's voice is a warning, but I don't care. Let them come at me. Better me than Grandpa.

"Autumn Leaves was a good idea. So thanks for that, Doc." See? I can play nice. Even if it's not true. "But you can tell those caseworkers up at the big house to leave us alone."

"We all want what's in the best interest—" Dr. Hirschman begins, addressing Mema and Mom instead of me or Grandpa.

"No you don't!" It's not a yell, but it's not *not* a yell either.

"Ellie! That's it!" Mom stands. "Out in the waiting room. Now." Mom gets quieter the madder she gets. She's at a low rumble. But I'm not done.

"I've seen that place—single rooms, one hospital bed and a toilet. Where's he going to put his favorite chair? What about his instant coffee? He likes to do it himself, and he and Mema are the only ones who know how many scoops to scoop!" I'm rolling back and forth in my chair like Pac-Man stuck in a corner, but I can't stop. "And what about Mema? I didn't see a lot of double beds in that place. Are you telling me she's gonna have to get a visitor's pass to see her own husband?"

Mema bangs her hand that holds the tissue on the top of Dr. Hirschman's desk. "My granddaughter is right," she says in a voice that is so much lower than a rumble, it's almost inaudible. "You want what's in his best interest? He stays with me."

Yessssss. I stop fidgeting. Mema's in it now. She's got this. I learned my fighting skills from her, after all.

"Mom—" my mom begins.

Mema waves a hand back toward us. "Alice, you will let me say my piece. Dr. Hirschman, I am not leaving Jonah." She gathers her purse and stands. I squeal so loud in my head I'm sure dogs can hear it. Victory!

Then Grandpa looks up at Mema. He taps her on

the elbow and smiles politely. "Can you help me find my wife?"

The question sucks all the air out of me in one whoosh. Mom gasps. Hirschman closes his file. Mema is a statue. No speaking. No breathing. She has just . . . stopped. I reach for her hand. The movement startles her, and she steps away from me, toward Grandpa. My arm falls.

"Jonah, honey, it's me." She touches his face. "It's Marianne."

He pulls back. Shakes his head. "No. My Marianne has hair as dark as the horse I rode up to her on the first day I saw her. She's a spitfire!" He smiles and then frowns and points a bony finger at her. "Listen, old woman, what are you tryin' to pull?"

He's called Mema "old woman" before, but it's usually playful—a joke they are in on together. But this is mean and ugly, and Mema begins to cry. It starts as a hiccup and turns into a moan. I've never heard a person make a sound like that. I dig the heels of my hands into my eyes to hold back the tears. I didn't know a sound could hurt so much. This whole *room* makes me hurt. The way Grandpa looked at Mema makes me hurt. The memory of him holding the baking sheet over his head makes me hurt. Everything hurts.

Mom rushes past me, jostling my chair to get to Mema

so she can lead her by the elbow out the door. They exit. About five seconds later the room fills with a musty smell. I look up but can't place it until Dr. Hirschman pulls back Grandpa's chair. "Come on, Jonah," he says, "let's get you cleaned up."

My grandfather has wet himself. There is a damp patch on his pants when he stands. He doesn't seem to notice.

I am left in a room that smells like the dining hall at the big house, like pee and sadness. Of all the things Grandpa has forgotten, he has never forgotten Mema. Until now. Alone, I let myself cry.

Keith groans from the desk behind me. Mrs. MacKenzie is passing back the in-class essays we wrote last week. How am I supposed to sit here in English class and pretend I care when an hour ago I was on the seventh floor of the hospital office tower watching my grandpa forget his life? Being a kid is just one whiplash moment to another—*Hey, sit for an hour and write this really long paragraph about a poem you didn't understand! Okay, now mix these two chemicals together and don't forget your safety goggles! By the way, there's corn on the cob with lunch, sorry you just got braces! Oh, you didn't sleep last night because someone in your family is in crisis? Too bad, time to play battleball!*

"Nice job," Mrs. MacKenzie says to me as she lays

a sheet of lined paper on my desk. Her face is a sea of wrinkles when she smiles at me. I nod because I don't trust myself to speak. Mrs. MacKenzie is a feeler. She always wants you to show your emotion in writing and in real life. But I'm a doer. When something makes me feel a way I don't like, I change it. Why talk about it? Fix it or get over it. "You're a good writer, Ellie," she adds. "You have a way with words."

What's the point of that if you can't convince anyone of anything in real life? I think. But what I say is "Thanks," so she'll go to the next desk and stop trying to read my mind behind her bifocals. I stuff the paper in my bag without looking at it.

After class, I feel Bert walk up behind me before I see him. My wheels start pulling to the left, toward him, without my permission.

"What did you get?" he asks, because he is also in Mrs. MacKenzie's class. I managed to make it through the whole period without looking at him. I still don't look at him, even as the halls fill and begin to funnel us toward our lockers and outside because it's the end of the day.

"Don't know." I push once, harder, and pick up the pace. Bert jogs to catch up.

"Seventy-eight point five for me," he says, even though I didn't ask. "The point five was"—he pauses, and I go faster through the doors until I am outside, sucking in cold air—"lack of title creativity!" he shouts, because I am so far ahead of him now. He catches up anyway when we reach the loading zone, and I have nowhere else to go.

Coralee is hopping up and down in her glittery silver Uggs to keep warm. "Dude? You got a seventy-eight?" She laughs and taps his forehead with her mittened hand. "Where's the big brain when you need it?"

"Point five. It was a seventy-eight point five." Bert rubs his forehead. They start talking again, but it's white noise to me, a buzzing in my ears that can't drown out Grandpa shouting "Old woman!" at Mema, until two words cut through the hum: "Brighton Academy."

"Brighton Academy is primarily a STEM school," Bert explains to Coralee, "but that doesn't mean they don't value a well-rounded liberal arts education. In fact—"

I spin around so fast, both Bert and Coralee jump back.

"Shut up already about your stupid school!" I yell. "Clearly, we're all not good enough for you now." I wave my arms at the one-story redbrick building and the cracked sidewalk and the yellow grass. "So stop reminding us!" I should stop talking. I should. But the part of my brain that knows that isn't connected to my mouth right now. I'm tired of thinking so many things no one wants me to say. "Apply for your stupid scholarship. Go to your stupid school. Get on with it already!"

Behind us, the entire basketball team erupts in applause over my speech as their bus pulls up for a game. Cole claps the loudest. I have done something to make Cole cheer. I'm hot and dizzy and cold at the same time. I can't feel my cheeks.

Coralee's mouth falls open. For once she doesn't have any words. And Bert—Bert's face has gone pale and blank, like the double-zero domino that's supposed to be lucky but always feels like a loss when you draw it. He won't even look at me. I want to throw up, but I burst into tears instead.

7

The More the Merrier

Dear Joy the Baker,

I hope this letter finds you well and that your winter in New Orleans is being kinder to you than ours here in Oklahoma. For Christmas, I got some special gloves with rubber grips to use with my wheelchair. They are coming in handy on these single-digit days.

Please say hi to your cat Tron for me. He seems much nicer than my friend Coralee's cat. We're pretty sure she ate one of the cockatoos, but they zoom around the trailer so fast it's hard to get an accurate count.

Anyway, I'm not here to talk about the weather or cats. I have a question. You know I love all your recipes because I've written to you about them before. Though I don't know if you read these letters or not. I hope so, but no pressure. I like to write them even if you don't read them. I wanted to ask you about one recipe in particular—your single-serving cinnamon roll. First of all, it is a thing of perfection. The center has the exact right amount of goo and the cream cheese glaze is melty, sugary bliss. You are absolutely right—it's totally worth it to take the time to make this tiny yeasted circle of excellence. And I am all about celebrating my independent, don't-take-attitude-from-anybody self.

But my mema always told me food was meant to be shared, and up until now I've agreed, because she tends to be right about most things. Except it's looking like my life is going to see a quick downturn in people soon. Seriously, Joy, the table is about to be sparse. I like being alone, but only when I get to pick. I don't think I'm going to be given much of a choice about it now. You say this cinnamon roll is a luxury to treat yourself. But is it still a luxury if I'm making it to prepare myself for when everybody leaves?

Sincerely,
Single-Serving Ellie

"I think you punched that thing enough." Coralee recrosses her legs where she sits on top of our yellow kitchen table.

"I'm not punching. I'm *kneading*."

"Well, you *need* to chill out for a minute and talk to me about your global meltdown in the parking lot today."

I slather the dough in butter and cinnamon and sugar, roll it up, nestle it in my smallest pan, and drape a dish towel over it to let it rise. *Then* I turn and face her.

"Grandpa forgot who Mema was today." Every word pricks with hurt.

"Oh. Oh no." Coralee hops off the table and pulls up a chair so we are eye to eye. She doesn't hug me, though, thankfully. She knows I don't like to be touched when I'm upset.

I rub my eyes with my wrist because my hands have flour all over them. Tired and sad is the *worst* combination. "And the doctor officially said he should move to the big house," I add. It's easier to get it all out at once.

"But your grandma and your mama wouldn't let that happen, right?"

I shrug because I don't know. After today, everything's changed.

Coralee picks a fuzzball off my sweater and doesn't look at me when she says, "You probably shouldn't have yelled at Bert, though."

I jerk back and bump into the open cabinet where I keep all my baking supplies on the lower level. "Don't 'shouldn't' me, Coralee. You of all people."

She holds up her hands. "I'm not! Er, I didn't mean to. I just thought we were going to come up with a plan to figure out how and when to talk to Bert *together*."

"Talk to Bert about what?" Bert says from where he stands in the open doorway, satchel across his shoulder and hands in his pockets. His hair is covered in a light dusting of snow. My first instinct is to reach up and brush it off. *Why?* Ugh. I tuck my hands between my knees.

Coralee smacks him on the shoulder. "Don't sneak up on people like that. You about gave me a heart attack."

He turns to me, silently asking permission to come all

the way in. I nod and then count the tiles in the floor so I don't have to look at him.

He takes a seat like a normal human, unlike Coralee, who climbs back up on top of the kitchen table. He is so close to me, our feet are almost touching.

"You two were talking about me?" he asks, and suddenly this kitchen is blazing hot.

"We wouldn't have to talk *about* you if you'd talk *to* us," Coralee chimes in from her perch.

"We know about the scholarship application, Bert," I mumble. It was easy enough to yell in the school parking lot. I don't know why it's so much harder to admit it here in the quiet of the kitchen.

The silence ticks so long, I look up. He's staring at the floor now, or maybe at my milk-and-cookies socks that Mom put in my stocking this year. I fight the urge to tuck my feet behind my footrest. Instead, I nudge him with the left one—the milk half of the pair.

He nudges me back but doesn't speak. It's the most playful thing Bert has ever done, and I cannot handle it.

"Come on, Berto!" I laugh. "Speak!" I sound like the Holly Jolly Santa that dances on Mema's hallway table—loud and mechanical. It's too much for this small space, but it does the trick.

"I didn't tell you because I am not applying."

Relief bubbles up in my chest like the best fizzy drink, and it erases some of the weariness of the day. I have to fight a giggle, because that would be totally inappropriate while Bert looks so pitiful.

"Why not?" I ask, making sure the corners of my mouth stay in a nice even line.

"Because I won't get in."

"Say what now?" Coralee climbs down and squats in front of him. We are a tight circle.

"Only twenty-four percent of scholarship applicants are approved." He sighs.

"Dude." Coralee thumps his knee. "You're a smartie. You'll nail it!" Which is the exact opposite of the message she gave him when he told her his essay score this afternoon. But that's Coralee—the queen of mixed messages.

"Twenty-four percent of applicants get in, but only *three percent* get both merit and financial scholarships." He sighs like an old man. "I can't go if I can't get both."

Bert's parents may own Food & Co., but he is also the youngest of thirteen. It's why he lives on this side of the bridge instead of in town. It also means the only way he'll go to a school like that is if the school pays his way.

We all sit back. Even Coralee lowers herself all the way to the ground, like the gravity of the situation is just too much for her. I'm grateful when my timer rings and I have to turn away to put the cinnamon roll in the oven.

When I wheel back around and catch the look on Bert's face, the fizzy relief of a second ago evaporates. I want Bert to stay, but not like this. He can't give up before he's even started.

"Come on." I roll toward the back door. "We've got sixteen minutes and it's hot as blazes in here. Let's take this out on the porch."

They follow me into the frosty evening, because they have no choice. We all know the porch is the place where things get worked out.

We plop down on the orange-and-yellow-flowered rocking couch in the glow of light from the kitchen window. It creaks under our weight and begins to rock as we huddle for warmth.

I catch Coralee's eye over Bert's bowed head.

"We need a plan," I say, echoing her own words from last week, when "the plan" was to destroy Bert's attempts to get into this school.

Bert won't look up. I've never seen him like this. For as long as I've known him, he's been the rational one. Two years ago he made a PowerPoint on the weather patterns in our area to prove to Mom that this was the perfect climate for me so she would let us stay in Eufaula. This past summer he took lengthy notes on fancy-dress protocol for me and Coralee in the beauty pageant. He has also taste-tested my best and worst recipes. Through it all, he's kept calm and carried on. Until now.

The fish starts swishing in my stomach again. I want to take his hand and not let go. But if we're going to get Bert's Bertness back, I have to help him leave.

"Bert Akers, you are the smartest person I know," I say. "You can do this."

He shakes his head. The sight of his bare neck covered in goose bumps makes me shiver.

"It won't work. I won't get in."

"You *will*," Coralee chimes in from his other side. "With our help."

He looks up, his eyes red-rimmed in the kitchen light. "How?"

"You forget that you are in the presence of a pie bake-off champion."

"And a second-placer in the Little Miss Boots and Bows beauty pageant!" Coralee fluffs her hair.

"We are winners." I scoot as close to him as I can, so our arms are touching from shoulder to wrist. "And so are you."

I don't know if he believes me or not. But I believe me. I believe it with my whole heart. Bert can do anything he puts his mind to, because his mind is grade A, top-of-the-line, first-place material.

Before he can respond, my phone begins to sing "Blue Christmas."

"Come on, y'all." I haul myself into my chair and wheel toward the door before he can say no again. "Elvis says time's up."

Back in the warmth of the kitchen, I pull out the pan and we all stare down at the single cinnamon roll.

"I *might* share if you ask nicely," Coralee says, making a grab for it.

I smack her hand away and pull the cream cheese glaze toward us.

"We split it. Three equal parts."

"See, Bert," Coralee says, licking the knife when I hand it to her. "We can do math, too. Put your faith in us and the sky's the limit."

I chew my perfect bite slowly and watch his face. He doesn't give anything away. But he doesn't say no, either.

8
No Pressure

"Happy snow day!" I shout, and Mom winces. This morning, her hair is bigger than Coralee's on pageant day. She stands at the kitchen counter, holding her coffee mug like it's the only thing keeping her upright. It might be. Long after I went to bed, she and Hutch sat in the living room and debated what to do about Mema and Grandpa. I know this because I did not actually go to bed.

Instead, I crept down the hallway as quietly as I could, crossing my fingers that my wheels wouldn't squeak. Their faces shone red and blue and green from the lights of the Christmas tree that we still haven't taken down.

Mom wants Grandpa to move to the big house. Hutch wants whatever Mom wants, because he's still the newest voting part of this family and is Team Mom all the way. But Mema isn't budging, even after what happened at the doctor's. In fact, she's more stubborn than ever about staying put. Around midnight, Mom got really desperate and called my dad back in Nashville to ask for his advice as a lawyer.

I couldn't hear everything. You can only creep so far before the purple-striped wheelchair gives you away. But I heard enough. At one point, Mom whispered into the phone, "It was a nick on his arm and a Band-Aid, but what about next time? Or the time after that? What then?"

That's the thing about Mom. She always thinks in worst-case scenarios. I guess it's because of everything she went through with me when I was little. I got sick. A lot. I had seizures that made me shake and drool and then sleep for hours or sometimes days. I don't remember the ambulance rides, but Mom does. During one doozy of a seizure, they wouldn't let her sit in the back with me, so she had to ride up front. She watched me through the little porthole window the entire way. When the EMT said she needed to turn around and put her seat belt on, she said, "Try and make me." Try and make me! I love it when she gets tough. Except I don't want her to get tough now. I want her to let Mema have what she wants and let them stay together where they are. Or better yet, undo what we did in the first place and bring them back here.

It was a long night for all of us. I lay awake inventing a recipe to make me fearless. It had cayenne and cocoa powder and loads of butter. But I still don't think it would be enough to get Mom on my side. By the time the early-morning sun was glinting off the fresh snow, I decided to commit myself to a problem I *can* fix.

Hutch drags himself in, looking even worse than Mom. He hasn't shaved in days. He's got more hair on his chin than his head now.

"Coffee, black, extra bold," I say, and lean over the counter to pour him a steaming cup. I grin and toss some pepper jack cheese, his favorite, into the eggs I'm scrambling. Then I dish out the eggs onto three of Mema's daisy-rimmed plates, which are older than all of us, and nudge the butter toward them along with a basket of still-warm cranberry-orange muffins. I'm trying to butter them up, literally, for the favor I'm about to ask. I've got to convince Hutch and Mom to let me out of the house in this weather.

"Listen," I say, steepling my fingers over my plate just

like Dr. Hirschman did. Maximize the power play. Establish authority and control. I've been taking notes. "Coralee and I were planning to go to Bert's after school today, but since there *is* no school, we figured we'd go after breakfast. We've got, uh, a group assignment. We wanted to get a head start."

I blink sweetly at Mom. See, I can be a mature young adult. I'm basically ready for high school right now. Mom eyes me over her coffee. This isn't her first rodeo. She knows the only projects I've ever completed early are baking ones.

"It's below freezing and the roads are ice," she says.

"That's why we need Hutch to drive us in his truck." I turn to Hutch, who halts midway through a bite of cranberry-orange muffin. "If anyone can maneuver these roads, it's you!"

He chews slowly. Swallows. Looks at me. Then looks at Mom. He is at a tiny round table in a tiny yellow kitchen with two women, and now he's got to make a choice.

"I—" He coughs into his napkin and pauses to take a sip of orange juice. "I think your mother's right, Ellie. They closed school for a reason. We better stay put."

"Surprise, surprise, you agree with Mom," I mutter into my eggs. But Mom's got ears like a bat.

"You will treat Hutch with the same respect that you treat me, Ellie. We are a family now, and we have to work together."

I throw down my fork. "Fine! Then work with me here! Bert's house is *one mile* down the road. Stop being so scared of every bad thing that might happen!"

Her face crumples. I want to crawl under the kitchen table.

"Ellie—" Hutch begins in the exact tone Mom uses. Since when did he learn *that* voice?

"No, leave it. Ellie's right." She turns to him like she can't bear to look at me. "Will you go warm up the truck? See if it's safe to get out on the gravel?" He nods and excuses himself from the table.

Once he's gone, she says, more to herself than me, "I guess I can't keep you in bubble wrap. Much as I'd like to. I'll send your sled, too. Go have fun with your friends." She smiles, but her face is still crumpled. My chest aches with an unsaid *sorry*. It hurts to make other people hurt.

Bert's tiny town is the best place to wait out a snow day. Looking at it, you'd never know it used to be a shed that stored the riding lawn mower. Now it has a ramp he widened especially for me, and the inside is filled with an exact (Bert would say "almost exact") replica of the town, including Lake Eufaula, all the way out to our bit on the other side of the bridge. It's taken him years to perfect, with only one setback in sixth grade, when Cole and his buddies broke in and busted up one corner. Sometimes it feels like the world is split into two kinds of people: the ones who tear things down and the ones who build them up.

Today Bert has come prepared with space heaters for every corner and blankets and beanbags and . . . a projector screen?

He gestures to the beanbags and gives a polite bow, his woolly red hat bobbing. "Ladies, please take your seats."

As I get myself situated, he pulls the screen all the way down over the far window, blocking out the bright white light of sun reflecting off snow. Coralee plops down next to me on a green beanbag and pulls an unzipped sleeping bag over us both. "Please tell me we are not watching something made on a nature channel."

"We are not," he says, fiddling with the cords that snake from the projector toward his laptop. When the screen goes blue, he sits back on his heels with a satisfied grin. It's good to see him smile.

"I've put together a little presentation to familiarize

you with Brighton Academy as well as its requirements for admission."

"Happy snow day to all," Coralee deadpans.

"If you'd rather not—" Bert begins to close his laptop.

"No!" I have to say something before Coralee crushes all the hopes and dreams we revived last night. "We said we're all in. I'm sure this will be very useful information so that we can help. Right, Coralee? Thank you for taking the time to put it together."

Coralee gives me the side-eye. I have never been more polite or less sarcastic. I order my face to stay neutral. The last thing I need is for her to sniff out my maybe, probably, imaginary new feelings for Bert.

She rolls her eyes and crosses her arms. "If we're doing this, there better be snacks."

"Snacks! Yes! I have snacks!" Why am I yelling? I clear my throat and try again. "Bert, could you please hand me that bag?"

"I can and I will!" he says, excited to be back on the presentation train.

"Here, you pass out these." I shove three Styrofoam cups at Coralee.

"How come I don't get a 'please'?" she grumbles. I ignore her and unscrew the thermos of hot chocolate.

Once we're settled with hot chocolate and homemade mini marshmallows (the secret is agave syrup), I crack open a tin of peanut butter fudge and signal to Bert to begin. He clears his throat and clicks on the first slide.

"Brighton Academy was founded in 1853 and is one of the oldest boarding schools in the country." The picture on the screen looks more like a college than any high school I've ever seen. Redbrick buildings with tall chimneys and arched windows line up like LEGOs along a pathway shaded by yellow-leafed maple trees.

He clicks to the next slide, which shows an old-timey photo of men and women in horse-drawn buggies.

"Though originally founded by Quakers to ensure that their children received a properly guided education—"

"Bert, are you turning Quaker?" Coralee asks through a mouthful of marshmallow.

"—the school began admitting non-Quakers in the early 1900s and has since become increasingly diverse," Bert continues, ignoring her, because he knows, just like I do, that when Coralee is in one of these moods, if you give her an inch, she'll take a mile . . . and then some.

The next slide reveals the school in springtime. Pink-blossomed crabapple trees surround a—oh, you've got to be kidding me—pond complete with a boathouse and a crew team gliding in sleek boats across the water. I sink down farther into my beanbag and fish a piece of peanut butter fudge out of my molar with my tongue.

"Modern-day Brighton Academy prides itself on fostering a climate of self-discovery, where students can follow their passions with purpose."

There's that word again—passion. I wonder if they have baking classes or if this is strictly a rowing, nature-loving, PowerPoint kind of crowd.

"With an emphasis on forming well-rounded, philanthropic future leaders of society, Brighton Academy—"

"Phil who?" Coralee interrupts.

"Philanthropic," Bert repeats. "It means striving to promote the advancement of others by making the world a better place through innovation and investment of time and resources."

"Well, that was clear as mud," Coralee says to me. This time I kind of agree. He just said a whole lot of words that don't seem to add up to much.

"Yeah, what exactly—?"

"Which leads me to my next slide," Bert says, talking over me. *Ummm, what?* Ignoring Coralee is one thing, but he better not start that business with me. I am about to tell him this when a familiar image pops up on the next slide. It's the merit scholarship application. I lose my thoughts and my voice.

Bert pulls a laser pointer out of his pocket and aims it at the categories of interest. A red dot hovers over "Global Engagement."

"If I apply, I plan to focus on global engagement with an emphasis on environmental sustainability."

"What do you mean 'if'?" Coralee frowns at the exact same moment I fight a smile. This whole "promising to help but not really wanting it to work" thing is very confusing.

Bert sighs. "The application is due March fifteenth, and along with a submission of grades, it also requires the completion of an independent project researching your area of focus. And I have to write an eight-hundred-word essay on why this topic is important to me."

He collapses onto a beanbag, looking like he already lost, and it drags my heart back into the game. "Bert, you are a walking Google. You know more facts than any person on the planet."

"So no pressure then," Coralee says. I elbow her under the sleeping bag.

"You design this project with that graphing calculator you call a brain," I say, "and we will make sure your eye is on the bigger picture. We will make a philanthropist out of you. You just have to tell us how. Seriously, don't be afraid to order us around."

"Speak for yourself."

"Shut it, Coralee."

Bert sits up. "Well." He rubs his hands together. "First things first—we'll need to establish a protocol for ensuring the sanctity of the scientific method."

Whatever he just said would probably have been more impressive without the hot chocolate mustache, but he looks so happy I don't want to slow his roll by pointing it out. Coralee, however, has no problem with this.

"Dude, wipe your mouth and let's take a sledding break. Brighton will still be here tomorrow, but the snow might not."

She tosses the sleeping bag off us and throws open the shed door, letting in a blast of cold air that gets everybody moving.

Bert wipes his mouth on his sleeve. It's adorable, dang it. "Fine, but Ellie gets to pick the hill." He knows I've figured out all the places on his property that work with my adaptive sled. Then he offers me a hand. Beanbags are wonderful when you're in them, but getting out is a whole other animal. I shake my head, though, and muscle myself up into my chair.

If Bert is going to leave at the end of this year, I better get used to doing things without him.

9
You Can't Argue with the Facts

I wriggle my toes in my milk-and-cookies socks, then look over at Bert.

"Stars and Stripes, huh? Didn't know you were so patriotic."

He contemplates his feet propped up on the wall. We're both lying with our feet up and our backs on the rectangle of carpet that used to hold Mema's sewing machine. Before she moved to Autumn Leaves, my bedroom was the guest-bedroom-slash-sewing-room. I could rip up the carpet, but this matted patch is my favorite thinking spot.

"My sister gave them to me for Christmas."

"Which one?"

"This past one."

"No, Bert. Which sister?"

"Oh, Ruby Grace. She has an internship in DC this semester and has gone fully patriotic."

All of Bert's brothers and sisters are geniuses. If Bert doesn't get this scholarship, Mr. and Mrs. Akers should play the lottery. The odds are in their favor.

"Explain why we're doing this again?" He turns toward me and his hair flops over on his forehead. It's ridiculously adorable.

"Uhhh, it helps with circulation." I thump my heel on the wall to demonstrate. "Gets the blood flowing. Perfect for scholarship planning."

When Coralee texted that she couldn't make it because Bunny ate an entire box of Mallomars Susie had stashed under the couch, I almost told Bert not to come. But now I'm glad I didn't. I can totally do this. We are just friends with our feet up on the wall . . . six inches away from each other . . . planning our futures.

I put my hands on my stomach and breathe. "So tell me about this project you want to do."

Bert holds his laptop up over our heads so I can see the website on the screen. "It's called silvopasturing."

"There is no way that's a real word."

"It most certainly is—from the Latin 'silvo' meaning 'forest' and 'pasture' meaning 'to eat' or 'graze.'"

"Oooookay. So what does it mean?"

"Did you know that one of the top ten solutions for climate change is the restoration of tropical rain forests?"

"Shockingly, I did not."

"Well, it is. And silvopasturing is one of the proposed solutions. It involves introducing livestock to land formerly used only for growing crops, as well as to forested areas—places that are normally cleared to make room for soybeans or corn or whatever crop the farmer seeks to grow."

"So you just mush the cows with the corn with the trees all in one spot? How does that help?"

Bert sets his laptop down and cups his hands together between us to form a circle. "It's a beautiful cycle. Animal waste boosts the growth of plants, and plants absorb gases from the animals that could be harmful to the environment."

I make a circle with my fingers to match his. "And the trees get to live happy and free."

"Exactly!" He grabs my hands in excitement and I freeze, which makes him freeze. We are statues in a sewing square surrounded by the clatter of squirrels darting across the roof. Bert breaks first. Was it my imagination, or did he hold on for a second longer than necessary? He clears his throat. "Isn't science amazing?"

Right, science, the whole reason he's here. I point at the laptop. "So that's silvopasturing, huh?"

"Yes—essentially, it is the belief that the things we thought we needed to keep separate work better together."

Suddenly, I am a fan of science.

"Hey, hey." Hutch cracks the door open. "Your mom's picking up dinner on her way home from visiting your grandparents."

"Okay," I say. Hutch continues to hover.

"One hour," he adds.

"*O*-kay."

Still no movement.

"Well, thanks, then," I say. How do you dismiss your physical-therapist-slash-gym-teacher-slash-stepdad?

"You need a ride home, Bert?"

"No thank you, sir. I'll walk. Both Albert Einstein and Charles Darwin walked daily. They believed that movement of the body frees the mind."

"That's one I can get behind," Hutch says, and chuckles awkwardly to himself. When Bert and I don't laugh, he steps back, shuts the door, and then reopens it a couple of inches before leaving. *Finally.*

"How is your grandfather?"

My brain glitches at Bert's question. It takes me a minute to jump from silvopasturing to accidental hand holding to grandparents.

"Oh, uh, same."

"Same is good, right?"

I shrug and rub the nubby carpet with my thumb. "Same isn't good according to his doctor and the people at Autumn Leaves. They want to move him to the main nursing home facility."

He nods—*nods!*—like he's not surprised. Does he think that's what should happen? We've *always* been on the same page when it comes to Grandpa. My heart thumps once and then lands like a wet pancake on the floor.

I push myself up until I'm sitting. It feels good to tower over someone. I glare down at him so I won't cry.

"Time for you to head out." I shove his legs. His American flag feet slide down the wall. He sits up and looks at me.

"You're angry." He blinks.

"I'm fine." I am not fine.

"You think he should stay where he is."

"I think he should never have left here in the first place! He was better off with us. He had more good days than bad when we were all here under one roof and he was surrounded by everything and everyone he knew." I shove down the guilt that rises when I think about how I let them move him in the first place. This place was his *home*. It still would be if I had fought harder.

Bert looks around my room. The closet that used to hold sewing boxes and wrapping paper is now filled with my clothes. The double bed has been traded for a queen. The arm bands Hutch has me use for stretching are tossed over my desk like rubbery snakes. It's all mine, yeah, but the bones of the place are 100 percent Grandpa's.

"He bricked this trailer himself. He built that porch. He made a life here." I throw up my hands. "He needs to get back to it. And Hutch has made this place completely handicapped accessible. It's already ready for whatever he needs!"

"They won't listen to you."

What's the thing parents always tell kids to say instead of "hate"? "Dislike." That's it. Well, I *seriously dislike* Bert right now. I pull myself into my chair and wheel toward the door I'm *glad* Hutch left open.

I pretend to check the time on my phone. "You've got a walk ahead of you."

He doesn't budge.

"They won't believe you, so—"

"Yeah, I got it. Thanks."

"So you have to prove to them you're right."

I pause at the door. Say what now?

Bert gathers his laptop and satchel and stands.

"Use the scientific method. Based on your prediction that your grandfather's mental, emotional, and physical health will improve here, design an experiment to gather and analyze data. When the time is right, you can present your argument with proof and appropriate conclusions."

I hold up a hand because I am still catching up. Here I was thinking Bert was using his super-logical brain against me, but really he was using it to help me win. "Let me get this straight. You want me to experiment on my family?"

He shrugs and pauses in the doorway. We are closer than we were on the floor. He smiles. "You can't argue with facts."

10

It's Dinner, but It's Science

Dear Campbell of the Campbell's Soup empire,

Are you a Mr. Campbell? Or maybe a Mrs. Campbell? Is there still a Campbell in a kitchen somewhere wearing an apron or are you a robot in a warehouse?? I hope not, because today I am writing to tell you a story that only a human would get a kick out of.

So, I have a very important dinner coming up. Life-changing, you could say. And the meal has to be a perfect blend of nostalgia and feel-good vibes. I need to make the people who eat it remember all the good moments they had when they ate that same dish before, right here, in this place. So I thought I'd make my grandmother's famous green bean casserole along with salmon patties and fried okra.

Do you know what my grandmother said on Thanksgiving a few years ago when I asked her for the super-secret recipe for this famous green bean casserole of hers? She said, "Oh, honey, I just use the one on the back of the can." And she laughed! Then she handed me a can of your cream of mushroom soup and sent me on my way.

I was skeptical, to say the least. I mean, creamed soup that slips out like snot and (if I'm being totally honest) smells a little like it, too? But you know what I discovered after two test batches? She was totally right. Your green bean casserole recipe with cream of mushroom soup and soy sauce and French's Crispy Fried Onions on top is the only way to go! So thank you, Mr. or Mrs. Campbell or generic factory robot, for making this family dinner the best it can be. Here's hoping it does what it's supposed to.

Sincerely,

Ellie

PS I am not a bot, I swear, so I hope this email doesn't get lost in your spam. I'm attaching a picture of me wearing an apron right now to prove it!

"You can't say no. I already dug through the pantry and meal prepped! And Mema said yes."

Mom turns so fast that I bump into her in our narrow hallway. "You already invited them over? *Without* my permission?"

"They're my grandparents! Since when do I need your permission?" Play innocent. And if worse comes to worst, act first, apologize later. I'm not apologizing *yet*, though, because this is the right thing to do, the *only* thing to do.

Mom grimaces like she just bit into a rotten grape, the ones that look like shriveled toes. I knew she'd be like this. It's why I called Mema in the first place.

I did it from the sanctity of my bathroom, which is one of my favorite places in the trailer, maybe the whole wide world, since Hutch and I knocked out the walls and made it *huge* and accessible for my chair. I stocked it with lavender candles and bath bombs. I even hung some pictures of the ocean that I found at T.J. Maxx. I named it Ellie's Serenity Palace, because it is basically a spa. It was the only logical place to make a potentially stressful call.

So last night, I lit a candle, held my breath, and dialed Mema.

"Hey, girlie. What's shakin'?" she asked in her singsong voice.

Thank the Lord. I let out a whoosh of air that almost blew out the candle. Jokey Mema meant Grandpa had a good day.

"I'm just relaxin' in the palace."

"You used any of those bath salts I gave you?"

"Yes, ma'am."

"Five ninety-nine at Mapco. Can you believe it? There were bath salts and eye masks right next to the roller rack of hot dogs!" Mema loves gas station shopping. Why go anywhere else when you can get everything from motor oil to pimento cheese in one place?

I touched the window and rings of fog bloomed from the heat of my fingertips on the cold glass. That was how I always used to figure out what to wear to school before I had a phone to check the temperature. If the window made my fingers tingle, it was a jacket day.

"Supposed to be below freezing again tonight, huh?" I asked, stalling for time. Now that I had her on the phone, I was getting nervous she'd say no.

"I know you didn't call to talk about the weather. Whatever thought you're chewing on that's got you hiding in the bathroom and calling your old grandma, you better spit it out right now."

"I want you and Grandpa to come over for dinner Friday night!" I whisper-yelled into the phone.

The silence on the other end ran so long I checked to see if my battery had died. Hutch cheered from the living room—one loud "yes!" and a clap. The Sooners must have scored.

Mema was the key to the whole plan. Without her, there *was* no plan. I bit the corner of my thumb where the skin was dry. "You still there?"

"Yeah, I'm still here, baby girl. I'm just thinkin'."

She'd never been one to make a hasty decision. I knew that. It didn't make the wait any less torturous. I tapped out a rhythm on the windowsill to give myself something to do. *Tappety-tap-tap* turned into the Johnny Cash song that Grandpa used to shuffle his feet to in the kitchen. Something about a "train a-comin'." He'd start slow and get faster and faster until he was practically running in place, and then he'd wheel me through the trailer like we were in a race. It scared the wits out of Mom. But he was the one who taught me my chair could be fun. This plan *had* to work.

"They still let you out of that place, right, Mema?" I asked, my voice a too-small thing in a too-big space.

"Yes, Ellie Cowan, last time I checked they haven't barred up my doors."

"So you don't have to sign in and out? They don't need to tell you if you can go?"

"No one's told me whether I can come or go since I learned to tie my shoes. You think your mema's ready to be put out to pasture just yet?"

I smiled into the phone. She was nice and huffy. Good.

"Not *just* yet."

"Friday night, you said?"

"Yes, ma'am."

"And you asked your mama?"

"I will. Soon."

"There's not much 'soon' left. Last time I checked, Friday was *tomorrow*."

"I know, I know. I just figured if I got you on board first . . ."

"You figured I'd team up with you and we'd steamroll her together."

I nodded even though she couldn't see me. My reflection in the mirror looked guilty. But I wasn't. I was *not*.

Mema clicked her tongue. "That's not how this family works, and you know it. We don't lie to each other, even if the truth's an uncomfortable one. Truth usually is."

"It's not a lie, exactly. I'm just not telling her yet."

"A lie of omission is still a lie. You tell her by tomorrow morning or I'm out. You hear me?"

"I hear you."

When Mema hung up, I kept staring at myself in the mirror. I had no reason to feel guilty about any of this. If I was going to prove to Mom that Mema and Grandpa were better off here, then I had to *get* them here to show her how wonderful it is. I was doing what was absolutely necessary to get this experiment underway.

At least, that was what I told myself last night. Now, though, in the early-morning darkness of the hallway, with Mom rubbing worried circles on her head, I'm not so sure. When she falls into a squat, I feel more like a criminal than a scientist.

I nudge her foot with mine. "I'm sorry I didn't ask you first. I thought you'd say no."

She sighs and sits all the way down on the floor next to my chair. "I probably would have."

"*Why*, though? When they first moved to Autumn

Leaves, we used to have them over after church on Sundays. Even though I think Pastor Clark is about a decade late on retirement, I still liked seeing them all dressed up in their Sunday best and watching Grandpa pretend to steal money out of the collection plate *every* time."

She laughs. "Every time."

"So why'd we stop?"

"I don't know, El. It got harder to get your grandfather to leave the condo. He gets agitated when his routine is changed."

"That's even more of a reason to have them over! We need to get him back in the routine of coming here and eating with us. You always say family is the most important thing, right?"

She rolls her eyes. "I do say that, don't I?"

I lean forward so we are eye level. "Please." Scientists wouldn't have to beg their subjects to participate. But who are we kidding? I'm no scientist. I'm just a girl trying to superglue her family back together.

Mom sighs again and holds out a hand so I can pull her up. "Six o'clock. They like to eat early."

"Yes! Okay! Six it is! Or if that's too late, I can do five or even four thirty if that would be better. It'll be like the British teatime!" Stop talking. Stop talking before she takes it all back.

"Six is fine, Ellie."

When I text Mema a thumbs-up, she responds with a fist bump, and we are back on track. I hum "I hear the train a-comin'" all the way to school.

I spare a second I don't have to check the clock on the wall. 5:37 p.m. I may have overpromised on the six o'clock start time. The kitchen is a mess. I decided to make biscuits at the last minute, and now the dough sits in a wet glop on the counter, still needing folding and cutting, and I've got lard in my hair. The green bean casserole is bubbling nicely in the oven, though, and the salmon patties are shaped and ready to be fried.

Right as I'm pulling the casserole out of the oven and putting in the biscuits, the kitchen door swings open and Mom walks in with Grandpa shuffling behind her, Mema at his heels. It's a flurry of activity as everyone shakes off scarves and coats. This kitchen is too small for a flurry of anything right now.

"Hi and bye! Y'all get out so I can get this done."

"Don't boss," Mom says, but she's laughing. This is the happiest I've seen her in weeks.

Mema gives me a real-life fist bump as she follows Mom into the living room, where Hutch hovers over the appetizer. It was all I could do to keep him out of it until they got here. Hutch would sell his truck for a fried pimento cheese ball.

I think Grandpa's going to walk on by with the rest of them, and I roll back to give him some extra space. He's more unsteady on his feet than he used to be. But he bends down and wraps his bony arms around me in a tight hug. His flannel shirt is cold against my cheek from the outside air, and he smells like cinnamon from the flavored toothpicks he always carries in his front pocket. I close my eyes and breathe in deep.

I only have to help him a little when he stands. "I hear we're in for a feast," he says.

"It's gonna be epic."

"I wouldn't expect anything less from the master chef." Bert says the aim of every good experiment is to gather data that supports your argument. As far as I'm concerned, this is proof enough. The night is already a success.

"Dinner in fifteen-ish minutes!" I shout, and shimmy on back to the stove to fry up some fish.

We are gathered at the table a mere thirty-six minutes later and I'm breaking open a steaming biscuit when Grandpa reaches for my hand. He takes Mema's in the other. After a split second, Mom and Hutch catch on and we all take hands. We aren't usually the pray-before-you-eat kind of people. Mostly because we've gotten too busy. We're either eating on the way out the door or scraping stuff together at nine o'clock at night. But Grandpa always blessed our meals when I was little. This is nice. He's back at the head of the table where he belongs.

He closes his eyes and clears his throat. We all bow our heads just like we've done hundreds of times at this very table.

"Good food," he begins in that deep voice of his. It calms me all the way to my bones. "Good food," he says again, and I get a little less calm. The pause runs so long after this that I peek at Mom, who's peeking at Mema, who's watching Grandpa with scrunched eyebrows. Hutch is the only one with his eyes still closed, but I see him squeeze Mom's hand. "Good food," Grandpa repeats for a third time.

"Jonah—" Mema begins just as Mom says, "Dad—"

His eyes pop open and I shut mine tight for fear of the look I'll see on his face. Then he shouts, "Good food! Good meat! Good God, let's eat!"

Every last one of us sighs, exasperated and relieved at the same time. Grandpa hasn't forgotten himself. He's remembered his sense of humor.

"Aww, I'm just messin' with y'all," he says, and picks up his fork like it's no big deal that he just gave the family a collective panic attack.

Mema swats him shakily with her napkin.

After a beat, Hutch nods. "Nice one."

"Thank you, son," Grandpa says.

Color rushes back to Mom's face, and she beams at the word "son."

Everybody begins to dig into the food, but my stomach is still churning from the bad turn this night almost took. Even though it is the most unscientific thing I could do, I shoot up a quick prayer of my own. *Dear God, please work a miracle and make this dinner a triumph. I need to bring my grandpa home for good.*

And it *is* a miracle, because an hour later I am ladling peach cobbler into bowls while Mema fishes the dominoes out of the china cabinet so we can play chicken foot while we eat our dessert.

As I pass around the tub of vanilla ice cream, Mema asks, "Are these the peaches we canned from the trees out front?"

"Yep, I thought I'd give us all a taste of summer in January."

"We had no idea what we were doing when we planted the first tree," Grandpa says now, holding up a peach slice shimmering with sugar and cinnamon. "Not a single peach for two years. We thought we'd gotten a dud!"

Mema chuckles. "The farmer didn't tell us you needed a *pair* of trees to get any fruit."

"Nobody can do it alone. Not even trees! Right, Marianne?"

Mema pauses in her shuffling of the dominoes. The look she gives him is better than any five-star meal. "That's right, Jonah."

When Mom drives Mema and Grandpa back to Autumn Leaves, I push up my sleeves and tackle the mass disaster that is the kitchen. I don't mind, though. I think best elbows-deep in a soapy sink.

I review the night. Mom didn't rub her head once. Mema said my salmon patties tasted just like hers. Hutch was a good sport when he lost all his toothpicks in chicken foot. And Grandpa—Grandpa never forgot himself once.

I took Bert's advice and set out to prove, using science, that my grandfather is better off at home than any place in the world. But what happened tonight wasn't science. It was pure magic.

11
Priorities

"**I can't believe we have to do this *every month*,**" Coralee grumbles the Monday after my epic Friday night dinner with the grandparents. She is nothing but two blue eyes and a red nose burrowed in her silver puffer. "We have just entered the soul-suck that is February. I *needed* those extra fifteen minutes."

"Research shows that rising before dawn can negatively impact your circadian rhythm. So in this instance, I agree with Coralee," Bert says, sipping coffee from a Yeti mug as big as his face. It smells like hazelnut. Normally, I would ask for a taste, but now the thought of putting my lips where *his* lips were is . . . confusing.

"Oh, you just had to add 'in this instance,' didn't you,

Robert." This early, even Bert agreeing with her won't make Coralee happy.

"Hello, Lakeview Larks! Thank you for joining me today!" Mrs. Rutherford chirps from center court. Someone's had more than her fair share of caffeine this morning. "Welcome to the second in our monthly series on paving the road to success in high school."

There are so many groans from the bleachers, the teachers don't even try to figure out who it is. In fact, I think a few of the groans came from their direction. Mrs. Rutherford ignores it all. She's got the best selective hearing of any adult I've ever met. It's probably why she's been principal for approximately 1,080 years.

"Today's theme is identifying and following your priorities. Can anyone tell me what a priority is?" No one speaks. It is three hours too early for class participation.

"A priority," Mrs. Rutherford continues, "is what you decide is most important in your life."

"If I say sleep is my priority, does that mean I get to skip the next morning assembly?" Coralee whispers. Everyone knows you can't whisper in a gym. The acoustics will get you every time. Mrs. Rutherford zeroes in on Coralee and clip-clops over on her sensible heels to ask, "Would you like to share one of your priorities with the group?"

Coralee stands, takes the microphone, and spins toward the bleachers. Uh-oh. I know that look. She's put on her pageant face. "One of my priorities is perfecting my star quality. Now, what I mean by that is my incredible combo of singing, acting, and dancing." She puts her hand on her hip, settling into the role. "As y'all know, I compete on the regular pageant circuit, and most of my competition also have the triple threat going for them. Which is why I've recently picked up guitar." She puts a hand over her eyes and peers into the crowd. "Does anyone happen to have a guitar?"

Mrs. Rutherford gently pries the microphone from Coralee's hand before anyone can answer. "Thank you, Coralee. That was . . . informative." Coralee does a quick curtsy in her puffer to a round of slow claps and sits down. Over by the doors, a few teachers laugh into their coffee cups. Mrs. Rutherford should have known better than to offer Coralee a stage.

"That was a wonderful, and thorough, example of identifying a passion and then turning it into a priority. A few more examples might be academic success"—shocker that she chose that one first—"or family or friends or music or art." Also no surprise that baking didn't make the list. Nobody thinks it counts unless you're Paul Hollywood bossing people around on *The Great British Baking*

Show. I love to bake, and it *is* my priority. But unless you get famous for it, nobody cares.

"However, ladies and gentlemen, your priorities aren't always what you think. You can say you love math"—more groans—"but if you choose video games over algebra equations, then your actions speak for themselves. So make sure that your priorities are reflected in how you spend your time."

Poor Mrs. Rutherford just lost the whole crowd. Even *I* would choose video games over algebra. Who wouldn't? Well, Bert wouldn't. But he's the exception. I look over at him. He nods along and sips his coffee like he's already in college. It makes me happy to see him happy. And also, it hurts. Because his priority is Brighton. I can't compete with that.

After Mrs. Rutherford dismisses us, Bert and Coralee and I wait for everybody else to file out. They know I like a clear path. But when Sierra comes down the bleacher stairs, instead of walking out with the rest of her crowd, she stops and fiddles with the zipper of her jacket. She just *stands there*, right in front of us, in her boots and tights and cool artsy patched denim jacket that I know Coralee secretly loves. I rock back and forth in my chair. Coralee and I could go, but Bert is still packing up, and something about leaving him alone with Sierra makes me itchy. Come on, Sierra. Get a move on.

"Hey, Bert," she says finally when he stands and throws the strap of his satchel over his head. He startles like he didn't know she was there. He probably didn't.

When he looks at me and then Coralee and neither one of us speaks, he says, "Hi."

"Yeah, hiya!" Coralee throws an arm around Sierra. It must have had some heft to it, because Sierra's knees buckle a little. "What's shakin'?"

"Oh, well, not much. I thought I failed the English test on citations, but Mrs. MacKenzie said—"

"Great, great." Coralee begins to steer her toward the exit, but in a genius acrobatic move, Sierra ducks, swivels, and is back to Bert.

"I heard you were applying to a boarding school!" She shouts it, probably because she's still a little out of breath from her Coralee-escape. It's loud enough to draw the trolls from under the bridge, aka Cole and Jackson, who were waiting for her by the gym doors. They turn to us, but don't move . . . yet. Why is Sierra talking to Bert? Why is Bert smiling at her instead of telling her he has to get to class? Bert *hates* to be late.

"Where'd you hear that?" Coralee asks.

She turns to Coralee. "Uh, from you? You all were

talking about it in the library during study hall on Friday."

I glare at Coralee, and she shrugs. I *told* her she was being too loud.

Sierra looks up at Bert. When did he get so tall? "I just wanted to say I think that's really cool, and, uh, I hope you get in. I mean, I knew you were smart, but you're like *extra* smart."

"Thank you," Bert says in his polite customer service voice. It's the one he uses when he hands people their Black Forest ham at the deli counter. I smile.

"Uh, you're welcome. And, also—?" Sierra fiddles with a bracelet on her wrist. Aqua beads dangle from a green braid. She probably made it. She's the kind who can do that sort of thing and make it look artsy instead of like something straight out of the bargain bin at Big Lots. "Can you believe the Cupid Ball is less than two weeks away?"

Hold up. Why is Sierra bringing up the Valentine's dance? Out of the corner of my eye, I see Cole wave off Jackson and take a step toward us. I roll forward. I am half an inch from Bert's elbow. He doesn't answer, because Bert doesn't answer questions that aren't really questions. It doesn't seem to bother Sierra, who *keeps* talking. "Well, this is the first year my parents are letting me go with a date. . . ." She drifts off like there might be more. There better *not* be more.

She takes one step closer. My pulse picks up a notch. They are now standing less than a foot apart. "So . . . ," she says, and gives him a smile that would win first place in any one of Coralee's pageants. There's a buzzing in my skull that drowns out logic. I cannot just sit here and stare up at them like their kid sister. My chair moves before my mind can catch up. One swift forward motion and I clock her right in the knee with my armrest. She dances back with a yelp.

"Oh, I'm so sorry! Sometimes this thing just gets away from me." I smile so wide I feel it in my jaw.

"It's, uh, no problem." She rubs her knee and gives Bert a long look and a longer silence that I know she's hoping he'll fill with an invite to the dance. Instead, he points to her knee with his Yeti mug and says, "The nurse has ice packs." I snort as quietly as I can. Bert, always ready with a friendly tip.

She shakes her head. "I think I'll be okay. I better get to class," she says, and begins to limp away. I let out a sigh at the sight of her leaving. But right before she reaches the doors and Cole, she turns, gives him one last megawatt grin, and calls out, "Bye, Bert!"

After a short pause, Bert gives a confused wave and I

click my tongue like a disappointed teacher. Coralee tilts her head toward me.

As soon as Bert makes a left toward his first class, I veer right. All I want to do is get to math so I can pretend to listen while freaking out inside that Sierra just almost *asked Bert out*, but Coralee has other plans. She orders me into the bathroom, slams the door, and blocks the exit.

"What in the ever-loving world just happened?"

I point at the door. "That's a safety hazard."

"*You're* a safety hazard! You just wheelchair-checked Sierra!"

"It was an accident!"

Coralee points a neon-blue fingernail at me. "Don't give me that. You're a pro in that chair. That was no accident. You were quiet as a church mouse until Sierra brought up the dance." She pauses and her eyes go wide, and then she *smiles*.

I reverse toward the handicapped stall and start shaking my head.

"No. Nononononono! Don't say it!"

"You like Bert!"

I shut myself in the stall and lock it.

"No, I don't!"

She bangs on the door.

"Yes, you do!"

"Shut up!"

Her head pops over the next stall. With her earmuffs still on and that smirk, she looks like a deranged Christmas elf. "I will not shut up, until you admit that you have romantic feelings for our dear Bert!"

"Never!" I unlock the door and race toward the exit, but Coralee is one step ahead of me and throws her back against the door.

"Say it. Or I will tell your mom and Hutch that you used the last of their fancy wedding sherry for your cherries jubilee cake."

I hit the brakes, glare at her. She leans back and crosses her arms.

"I admit nothing."

"Come on!" She throws up her hands and walks over to the sinks. I could race out the door right now. But I don't. A *very* tiny part of me realizes it would be nice to have someone to tell.

She pulls off her jacket, spreads it on the floor, and sits crisscross applesauce on it like she's about to have a picnic right here in the restroom.

"Tell your auntie Coralee all about it, honey."

I sigh and lean back. "There's no 'it' to tell. I just . . . like Bert." There. I said it out loud. The words stick to my tongue like peanut butter.

Coralee nods. "Of course you do."

"What do you mean 'of course'? Stop smiling!"

"I just mean your weird and his weird complement each other. He likes facts and science and . . . manners. And you like arguing and baking and the opposite of manners."

I cross my arms. "So he's smart and polite and I'm good with food and rude? *That's* your argument for why we were meant to be together?"

Coralee grins. "You just said 'meant to be together' and you were talking about Bert."

"I *will* run you over."

"I just mean you two have always known how to talk to each other."

"What about you and me?"

"Well, sure. I'm in a category of awesome all my own. But Bert . . ." She pauses, searching for the right words, then snaps her fingers. "You know that look Francis gets when you rub between his eyes?"

"Yeah."

"That's what you're like when you're around Bert."

"Like I'm a bird who needs a nap?"

"No! Just . . . you're totally relaxed around him! He chills you out, is what I'm saying."

"Well, I am not chilled out right now."

Coralee smirks. "Of course not. You're in *like*."

"Thank you for not saying love."

She gets up and opens the door. "We'll save that for the second date."

"Hold up." I grab her by the tail of her sweatshirt. "I am never telling him and you better not either."

She holds up three fingers in the Girl Scout sign. No way she was ever a Girl Scout—they have to take an oath to respect authority. "I won't tell him. I swear. Because you're going to."

"Uh-uh."

"Sure you will. Unless you want to watch Sierra ask Bert to the super-duper dreamy *Cupid* Ball."

I visibly shudder. She points at me. "See."

She's right. If I have to watch Bert get dressed up on the worst holiday of the year and take Sierra to the most absurd extracurricular activity ever invented by middle school teachers, I will lose my ever-loving mind.

"I don't know how to tell him," I whisper.

Coralee hitches her backpack higher on her shoulder. "You'll figure something out. You always do."

12

Bake It Like You Mean It

Dear Ree Drummond, aka the Pioneer Woman, aka fellow Oklahoman, aka one of my favorite food bloggers ever,

    Let me start by saying that I am truly ashamed that I did not know you also wrote one of my favorite kids' books of all time. Charlie the Ranch Dog is the reason I begged my mom for a basset hound. She almost let me get one, too, but I was still trying to get the hang of my wheelchair back then and she was afraid he might topple me over. Come to think of it, I might ask her again, now that I'm a champ roller and we live in the country. It's not a ranch like yours, but it's enough space for him to run.

Speaking of your ranch, have you ever heard of silvopasturing? A friend told me about it, and it might be something to consider with your cattle. But it's not why I'm writing you today.

I wanted to ask you a question. It's a serious one. A romantic one. That friend I told you about is someone I kind of hope turns into more than a friend. You wrote once that nothing is more romantic than putting your feelings into a homemade treat. So here's my question: How do you know what treat is going to get your point across? Because when the time comes, I think I'd rather eat my own tongue than have to explain myself. I'd rather the food just speak for me, you know? It's my love language (hahaha).

I'm still not exactly sure what will do the trick, but I picked your famous Red Velvet Sandwich Cookies to give it a shot. It's almost Valentine's Day, and they seem especially festive. Also, they're cream-filled, and this person has a major sweet tooth.

Here's hoping my "friend" gets the message loud and clear. I guess if he doesn't, at least I'll have a batch of goodness to eat myself.

Your fan,

Ellie, aka the other Oklahoman baker

"Don't touch those!" I shout, and swat Hutch's hand with a dish towel before he can grab a cookie. He looks confused, as he should be. I always let him taste my test batches. But I've been fine-tuning these all Saturday, and I'm too worked up to have him mess about in my kitchen.

"Why not?"

"Because they're still cooling." I smile. Please let my face be normal.

"Well, save me one . . ." He follows the line of baking sheets that snake all the way from the kitchen into the dining room. "Or twenty."

"Testing is a detailed process!" They have to be *just* right. The first batch wasn't chocolatey enough. The second and third batches didn't puff up, and as for the fourth, well, it was a total disaster.

But these, though, these might be the ones. I study the perfectly rounded cherry-red cookies I've just taken out of the oven. They are impeccable, and the whole kitchen smells like warm cocoa and butter. How can you not love that? Or the person who made that? I swallow and chase the fear with a bite of cookie. Hutch raises an eyebrow but doesn't say a word. Now all I have to do is whip up the cream filling, pack them in the heart-covered baking tin, and get myself to Bert's—without throwing up from nerves along the way. Easy peasy.

Mom wanders in from the living room, where she was folding clothes. We expanded the laundry room so it's actually a room now and not a cubby with folding doors, but she still likes to fold on the couch so she can yell at the news.

"Ohhh!" She reaches for one.

"Don't touch," Hutch says, grabbing her hand and not letting go. "They're hot."

"Yes, they are," she says, and gives him a wink. Ewww. At least I know the cookies work on *somebody*.

"Hey, wasn't last Friday with the grandparents awesome?" I ask to interrupt the lovefest before I really do throw up all over these cookies.

"Yes, Ellie, it was. I already told you that when you asked the same thing yesterday and the day before that and the day before that." Mom breaks eye contact with Hutch long enough to steer a baking sheet farther onto the counter.

"I'm just saying, we should do it again soon. Seemed like everybody had a good time."

"Hmmmmm" is all she'll say—the universal grown-up sound for "we'll see," which usually means "no." I don't understand what her deal is. It went perfectly well.

"Why won't you let them visit?"

"I did."

"One time!"

"What do you want from me, Ellie? I am doing the best I can!" Mom throws up her hands. Hutch begins to inch his way out the door.

"I want you to stop worrying about every little thing that might happen and enjoy life for *one* second."

"I do!"

"Not when it comes to Mema and Grandpa."

"Ellie—"

I turn the mixer on high speed to drown out her words. Cookies, Ellie. Focus on the cookies—the one thing you *can* control.

Francis hops along the back of my wheelchair, feasting on bits of my homemade granola. I shouldn't be here right now. I should be on my way to Bert's. But I needed a Coralee moment to make me brave.

"Okay, give it to me. Don't hold back. I need the pep talk of all pep talks or I'm never going to do it."

Coralee begins to pace her floor like a leotard-wearing general. This is her moment. This is what she was born to do. I'm a little scared.

"Do you want to spend the rest of your life wondering 'what if'?"

"No."

She points one of her batons at me. "I can't hear you!"

"No!"

"Do you want to spend the rest of your life as 'friends' with someone who could be more?"

"Uh, maybe?" She shoots me a look. "What? It's better than totally losing that friend if he doesn't feel the same way."

"Okay, fine. Then do you want to spend the rest of your life kneecapping random women?" She holds the baton like a baseball bat and takes a swing. "Because that's what you'll want to do to anyone who so much as looks at Bert."

"Fine. No," I groan.

"Louder!"

"No!"

"Okay." She sets the baton down and scoops Francis off my chair. "Get on with it, then."

"I have a question." I point to her window, where Bunny sits outside, staring at us like the grim reaper. "What's going on there?"

"She tore up a pack of Susie's smokes. She's been banished."

"I'm surprised she's still alive."

We both look at her. She does not blink.

Coralee taps on the glass. "I'm not sure she is."

Because of my detour to Coralee's, it's later than I planned when Hutch drops me off at Bert's. It's getting dark out—the sky a gray going on black, but I spot Bert in tiny town with his back to the open door, laptop on his legs and his feet propped up on the miniature bridge crossing Lake Eufaula. He doesn't notice me at first. He is in deep Bert-concentration mode.

I pause at the ramp to the shed. I could leave. He'd never know the difference. It's not like this needs to happen *now*. But before I can reverse, the sound of Hutch's pickup engine revving in the drive as he leaves makes Bert turn around. He sees me. He smiles. I guess I'm going in.

My breath makes puffy clouds in the cold as I muscle

up the ramp, but once I'm in, the shed is nice and toasty with the space heaters going. The red velvet declaration of "like" cookies are in my bag, which is hanging from the back of my chair. I can feel them there, tick-tick-ticking down to the moment of no return.

But first, let's talk about the weather.

"Cold out, huh?" I ask.

He scoots over to make room for me on a beanbag. I consider staying in the chair for a faster getaway, but it looks so cozy and Bert's hair is adorably rumpled, so I sit.

"It's global warming. Most people think that makes the earth warmer, which it does, but according to a recent study, this warming, especially in the Arctic, can disrupt the polar vortex, making winters more severe."

"Is this what you do when I'm not around? Read studies and hang out in tiny town?"

I'm joking, but he tilts his head, thinks for a minute, then says, "Yes, and work behind the deli counter."

"Well, I'm glad I came to shake things up." I punch him on the shoulder like Coralee would do and it feels weird and my smile is frozen and can somebody remind me how to act normal, please? "Oh, I brought snacks!"

I point to the bag. Bert unhooks it from my chair and hands it to me. My heart is only beating approximately forty-five times faster than usual. I fumble with the lid of the tin. He takes it from me and opens it in one smooth motion. He does not notice the hearts on the outside, and I don't point them out.

The smell of chocolate and cream and sugar surrounds us like a hug and boosts my confidence. I'm in my element now.

I pass him a red velvet cookie that is flawlessly domed and filled to the brim with icing. It is both heavy and light in my hand.

He takes a giant bite, half the cookie, and I have to keep myself from ordering him to slow down and really taste it. I already know how it will dissolve in his mouth, first the cakey cookie, which is sweet, but not too sweet, and then the sugary middle with a teensy bite of tang from the cream cheese.

He closes his eyes and leans his head back against the wall. "These might be the best cookies I have ever eaten, objectively speaking."

I'm glad his eyes are still closed when he says it, because I can't hide my smile or the rush of heat to my face. I tuck my hair behind my ears. Coralee made me wear it down. It tickles my neck. For once I'm thankful for the darkness. It's now or never. I've got to tell him.

"I, uh, made them for you."

He opens his eyes and turns to me. "Thank you." Bert, always polite. He finishes the rest of that cookie and reaches for another one.

"You're welcome. They're uh, message cookies."

"They are?" He holds one up and checks the bottom, like there are actual words imprinted on the cookie. I want to crawl in a hole and hide. So much for the cookies speaking for themselves. Maybe I should have made fortune cookies and literally typed out: *You will fall for your best friend who has brown hair, likes to bake, and oh yeah, is named Ellie.*

"No, I mean, they come with a message." I gulp air and it scratches all the way down. "Bert, listen, I have to tell you something. It's—" Holy Moses, I cannot sit here on this beanbag when I say this. I need leverage. I pull myself up into my chair. "So, I think that you and I . . . I mean, if you want to . . . if you've even thought about it . . ." I am out of breath. It's too hot in here. I wish we could do this outside. I try again. "Think about us as an experiment. What if—"

Bert snaps his fingers and I jump. "That reminds me!" He wipes off his hands and pulls his laptop toward him. "Obviously it would be ideal to have data from an actual real-life experiment to present on silvopasturing." Bert runs his hand through his hair, making it stick up at all angles. "But the application is due March fifteenth. There's just not enough time. So I've been working on a silvopasture three-dimensional model instead."

He tilts his laptop up toward me so I can see the screen. I pretend to study it, but my heart is a thrown stone sinking to the bottom of the lake. The application, *of course*. For the school where Bert can go to be around people who understand whatever this is he's showing me on the screen. People who have read that same study on global warming. People who don't waste their time baking cookies. How could I forget?

"I hope you know I absolutely *cannot* pull off the essay portion without you," Bert is saying. "You are the wordsmith, after all. But I thought you might be interested in seeing this part as well."

I can't speak. Here I am talking about *us* as an experiment, while all he can think about is this one. Something pretty obviously catastrophic must be going on with my face, because when he looks from the screen to me, he says, "We could talk about the thesis of the essay, if you prefer. I have a decent claim, but it's still missing something. I'm just not sure what."

Oh, you are *definitely* missing something. I dig my nails into my knees and look at the screen longer than necessary, until it blurs and I have to blink. This whole thing was a mistake. He's never going to see me as anything more than someone who can bake a cookie and write a decent paper. I'll never be enough to make him forget himself like he does when he talks about Brighton.

My chest pinches like it used to when I would get pneumonia. But I'm not sick. I'm sad. Can you actually feel your heart when it breaks? I roll back from him and the glow of the screen so he can't see my face. "I—I don't think I can help you with your scholarship anymore." I shake my head when he opens his mouth. If he says one nice, kind thing about how good a friend I am to help him, I will totally lose it. "I'm sorry! I shouldn't have offered in the first place. It was a mistake. This—" I wave my hand at tiny town, with its cozy beanbags and humming space heaters and my "like" cookies sitting half-eaten in their heart tin. "This was a huge mistake." I back away. "I—I've got to go!"

I reverse, one wheel almost slipping off the ramp, but I make it down before he can stop me.

"Wait!" Bert calls from the doorway.

I look back. He is a tall, messy-haired shadow. I shiver under too-bright stars. I manage to wheel as fast as I can down the road and out of sight before I burst into tears and call Coralee. She and Susie come to the rescue in the Cadillac and fuss over me about being in the cold. But I don't feel it. I'm numb from the inside out. Coralee was wrong. Bert and I are not the kind of weird that goes together. We are the kind of weird that repels each other—two mismatched magnets pulled in opposite directions.

13
What a Mess

A week ticks by. I keep my head down at school. I get an A on another English paper, and Mrs. MacKenzie asks me if I'd be interested in tutoring some sixth graders. I tell her I'll think about it, so she'll leave me alone. I'm only good at words on paper, not with people in real life.

I manage to avoid Bert as best I can. I bury myself in homework at our lunch table so he won't talk to me, because he's polite like that, not wanting to interrupt. It's the same on the way home. The van would be as silent as a library if it weren't for Coralee's constant chatter. I could almost pretend he's not here, except I can feel him studying me sometimes, like I'm a Rubik's Cube he's trying to solve.

To distract myself, I bake boatloads of cookies and pies and cheesecakes and tarts—so many that I end up taking half of them over to Coralee and Dane and Susie, who don't complain because they're off the diet train now. I spend most of my time there, listening to Coralee practice guitar and swat at Bunny when she attacks the strings.

When I do have to be home and there's nothing left to bake, I sit on the couch while Mom grades papers and Hutch shouts at a basketball game that I pretend to watch.

Bert once told me that when a body is in motion, it stays in motion. But the opposite is true too. Once you stop, it's real easy to stay stopped. I float through, doing homework, hanging with Coralee, eating dinner with Mom and Hutch. But my heart's on pause.

Until Wednesday, when Bert doesn't show up to lunch.

"Where is he already?" Coralee asks, swiveling her head so far to the left and then the right that her neck pops. She is more flexible than a bendy straw.

"Why does it matter?" I eat a lukewarm bite of mac and cheese, but I'm grateful I packed my lunch since today's special is corn, corn dogs, and corn chips. I think the cafeteria workers are getting bored.

"Girl—" She pulls the container of macaroni away from me. "You have got to talk to him."

I steal my food back. "No, I don't. He's going to Brighton. It doesn't matter. I've already lost my best friend—"

"*One* of your best friends," she interrupts.

"*One* of my best friends, and—"

"And you haven't lost him."

"That's what you say, but—"

She holds up a hand. "I hope y'all have figured out who gets me in the separation, because I can't be doing this back-and-forth business."

"What back-and-forth?"

"You complaining in one ear about Bert not appreciating you and Bert asking in the other why you won't talk to him and what he did wrong! I'm dizzy with all the conversations you all *aren't* having with each other."

I lay my forehead on the table, which smells like old cheese and Lysol. "There's no way he'll forgive me for quitting. I can't believe I ever thought he'd like someone like me."

Coralee slams down her Dr Pepper so close to my head that I sit up. "Uh-uh. You *do not* dis yourself like that at this table. You are Ellie the Master Baker, and you are all-powerful. I will not tolerate that whiny attitude."

I'm about to tip over her Dr Pepper when Cole and Jackson strut into the cafeteria. They're laughing into their fists and staring at their phones. Then Cole's beady little eyes dart over to our table, to me, and he smirks. All the hairs on my arms rise on high alert. Something is wrong here. I nudge Coralee, who looks at them and then at me.

"Bert," we say at the same time.

I push away from the table and roll out the door, with Coralee close behind. But once we're in the halls, I don't know where to go. I grab my wheels and brake hard. Coralee gets a push handle in the stomach.

"Oof! Watch the sudden stops, E!"

"Which way?!" My hands want to move, but without a direction, I'm just hovering them over my wheels. My whole body vibrates like a windup car before you let it go. I need a direction! "Should we try the library?"

Coralee shakes her head. "No way. Everybody knows the library is the safe zone. It's like home base. You want to cause trouble, you find somewhere else to do it."

"Where, then?" I spin around. And then I spin around again. I am literally going in circles. And then I see it, way at the far end of the hallway, illuminated by the exit sign—Bert's satchel.

"Come on!" I shout, and we race toward the bag. It's intact but empty. There's no sign of Bert.

I'm hugging the satchel to me when I happen to look up and spot something crumpled and red next to the doors that lead outside. It's Bert's woolly hat.

We go slowly, Coralee first and then me rolling after. Two seconds ago I was jittery with movement, but now my arms hang heavy. I have to force them to move. I stop to pick up Bert's hat, and it hits me as I cup it in my hands—I'm afraid. I'm afraid of what we'll find outside. Jackson is basically harmless on his own, but he'll do whatever Cole tells him. Cole is mean—the kind of mean that kicks cats and grabs at girls and pretends it's an accident.

Despite Coralee being in front, I spot him first.

"Bert—" My voice breaks.

He is on his hands and knees in a puddle of vomit by the dumpsters. He doesn't look up. He doesn't move at all.

I freeze for a second, too; not sure whether he wants us to come or go. Then I decide I don't care, because I can't leave him like this. So I roll over and gently tug his hat back on. He lifts his head. His bottom lip is cracked and bleeding and his eyelashes are wet, from tears or the cold or both.

"Cole?" I ask.

He closes his eyes and nods. Then half sits, half collapses against a dumpster.

Coralee comes around to one side and I roll over to the other, so we are Bert's buffers against the cold.

"I'm going to make him wish he was never born," Coralee says.

Bert shakes his head. "It's not worth it." His voice is raspy and raw.

"At least let us tell a teacher," I beg.

"Don't," he says, and wipes his eyes with the back of his hand. "It'll just make it worse." I find a tissue in my pocket and he takes it and blows his nose, then tries to wipe a damp, sour-smelling patch off his shirt. The tissue dissolves in crumbly bits down his front.

"What happened?" I whisper.

When he doesn't say anything for the longest time, Coralee and I share a look. We don't know what to do.

"They told me Mr. Barlow asked us to empty the trash cans in the lab," Bert says finally. He picks at his nails. There's icy grit under them. He does not look at us while he talks. "We had just finished the lab on algae growth. They each had a trash can, so I believed them. But . . ."

"You don't have to talk about it if you don't want to," I tell him, and Coralee gives me an *are you kidding me?* glare over his head.

"It's fine. You might as well know. You'll hear about it sooner or later." He clears his throat. I swallow because it looks like it hurts. "When we got out here, they pushed me down and emptied my satchel in the dumpster. Then . . . then they showed me what was in the trash cans."

Coralee leans in, like it's the beginning of a scary story

you'd tell around a campfire, but I want to plug my ears. I'm afraid to know. Still, I nudge him so he'll keep talking, because not knowing doesn't make it not happen.

"I guess they found out I did not eat meat anymore. And that I was applying to Brighton. They said it sounded like I thought I was too good for them and their regular school and their regular food. The trash cans were full of old corn dogs soaked in creamed corn." He touches his lip. "They said if I didn't eat all of them, they'd smash my laptop. I ate as many as I could, but then . . ."

I glance over at the puddle of vomit and then quickly look away.

"I got sick."

He points to his laptop, sitting by the door on a slick of ice. "At least they kept their word."

Coralee smacks the dumpster with her fist. It makes a dull thud. "Yeah, truly noble."

I pass Bert his empty satchel, lock my wheels, and help him up. Coralee fetches his laptop.

"I'm going to get cleaned up," he says, carefully placing the laptop back inside the bag. He does not look at us when he leaves. Usually, it makes you feel better to talk something out, but before he disappears behind the closing doors, I watch his back and it is hunched and my own shoulders sag with the weight of all the sadness he carries.

Coralee keeps it together until he's gone, then launches into a list of all the things she is going to do to Cole and Jackson the second she gets her hands on them.

But I can't listen. If I hadn't avoided Bert all week, he would never have been alone on his way to lunch in the first place. Cole and Jackson wouldn't have dared mess with him with me and Coralee around. That's always been the magic of us. We are strongest together. My chest aches, but it's not from the cold.

I spend the rest of the day worrying over what to say to Bert on the way home after school, but he tells Hutch he doesn't need a ride. After Hutch drops off Coralee, I get him to make an unscheduled stop at Birch Street. Something in my tone must convince him it's important, because all I say is, "I need to talk to Mema," and he makes a U-turn past our trailer and back onto the road.

"I'll be here in an hour," he says once I'm settled in my chair in front of their door. He looks like he might hug me, but he doesn't. I'm glad. I think I might start crying if he did, and neither one of us would know what to do with that.

Anvi answers the door with a bright smile and a "Hey, Eldorado. Long time no see!"

We make small talk about school and her little brother, who's going into sixth grade next year.

"I tell him he's got nothing to worry about! Middle school's a piece of cake!" she says. I nod. A piece of cake. Sure.

Mema comes to the rescue a minute later, her long hair damp and hanging down to her waist. "I wasn't expecting visitors!"

"Sorry to interrupt your afternoon, Mema," I say, and she shoos me down the hallway after Anvi goes back to the living room, where Grandpa is napping in his chair.

"Don't you ever apologize for visiting me, sweet thing. It is the highlight of my day!" She closes the bedroom door behind us. She points to her wet hair. "I know Anvi's got an eye on him, but I still like to shower when your grandfather's napping, so I can be there if he needs anything when he wakes."

Her smile is bright but her eyes are tired. I wonder how much sleep she's getting these days.

"But"—she rubs her hands together—"now that you're here, I'm putting you to work." She hands me her round wood-handled brush. "I was just in the middle of my beauty routine."

I force a laugh. Mema's beauty routine consists of hair brushing, and that's about it. Dab on a little rose lotion and she's good to go. She had to borrow lipstick from Coralee for Mom's wedding.

Mema sits down at her dressing table. The mirror is so warped that we look like fun-house versions of ourselves—tall foreheads with fat cheeks and narrow chins. It stretches my frown into an almost-smile.

"To what do I owe the honor of this visit? I know you weren't just in the neighborhood."

I pause mid-stroke. I don't really know what I'm doing here. It's not like Mema can clean up the mess I've made of things with Bert.

"I guess I just needed to see you. I miss you."

"I miss you, too, baby girl."

"You know, if y'all lived at home, I could brush your hair anytime. And you could shower whenever you wanted. I'd keep an eye on Grandpa for you."

Mema closes her eyes and sighs. I can't tell if it's because the movement of the bristles through her hair is relaxing or because she's sad.

"Oh, honey," she says after a minute. "I'm just trying to keep us out of the big house. One thing at a time, huh?"

I nod. She's right. I can't fight all the battles at once, and the one I came here to talk about tonight is still hanging in the air like an angry storm cloud.

I fall into a rhythm with the brushing, pausing every now and then to untangle a knot with my fingers. It's calming in the way baking is. It gives me something to do with my hands.

"What would you do if you'd been a bad friend to someone?"

"Bad how? Are we talking gossiping or third-degree murder?"

"Closer to the first, but it feels like the second."

"What happened?"

I can't tell her everything. I don't want her to think I'm a bad person. I know family is supposed to love you no matter what, but I'm too embarrassed. I settle for the sound-bite version. "I quit on someone when they needed me most."

She turns to face me. "Are they fighting in a war or lost at sea?"

"Uh, no?"

"Then they are reachable, which means all is redeemable. You've just got to apologize."

My face goes hot with shame. "I can't."

"Why in the world not?"

"Because!" Forgetting I'm still holding the brush, I throw my hands up to cover my face and bang myself in the forehead.

"Lordy, El. Don't give yourself a concussion." She pulls my hands down and takes the brush away. "Whatever's going on isn't going to get better the longer it sits. It's not like chili. Hurts are best handled fresh. So swallow your pride and talk to your friend."

I nod, but in my head I'm screaming *I don't want to! I don't want to!*

"Listen, honey, I'm one to talk. Your old grandma is just as stubborn. But"—she squeezes my hand—"stubborn and strong aren't the same thing. Strength is being able to admit when you're wrong."

She's right. Bert might be going to Brighton in a few months or he might not, but either way I can't leave it like this. I grimace.

"You look like somebody just stepped on your tail." She swats me on the shoulder with her hairbrush. "Now get to work. Untangle this first and then go untangle whatever mess you made."

14
Born to Be Wild

Dear Tieghan of Half Baked Harvest,

Happy Valentine's Day! Or almost. I actually don't care for the holiday myself. My dad says it's a capitalist hoax meant to sell candy and Hallmark cards, but I think that's just because he forgets to buy my stepmom a gift. My stepdad is all about it, though. I found his pile of gifts in the china cabinet yesterday. I think he bought the entire display at CVS.

Anyway, I am currently making your extra-awesome Lunchroom Chocolate Peanut Butter Bars. You mention that this treat was one of the few good things about school for you in a big old sea of not-so-good things. I know you ended up homeschooling when you were around my age. I got to thinking about that while I was waiting for the bars to cool in the fridge. Was it better for you that you left? Or do you wish you'd stuck it out?

    I'm asking because my friend is currently in this position. School is rough for him, but he has the chance to go somewhere else and do something different. I haven't been very supportive. I feel bad about it. Terrible, actually. Your bars are part of my apology. I really do want what's best for him. But I also don't want him to leave. What I want and what I know is best are in a tug-of-war, and I'm stuck in the middle holding on to my peanut butter bars for dear life.

    I'm sure you'll say homeschooling was worth it, because it let you follow your passion and you are this hugely successful businesswoman and home baker. I guess that's why I wanted to ask you in the first place. I needed to know that leaving might be the best thing for my friend.

Now that I wrote all that, I kind of want to quit school and bake full-time. My mom might murder me if I did, though, so I guess I'll keep baking as an extracurricular for now.

Happy home baking,
Ellie

Bert is not at school on Thursday or Friday. He does not answer his phone when we call. Our texts go unread—even the SOS ones and the ones that are twenty-seven emojis long with no words. So Coralee and I really have no choice but to stop by Food & Co. on Friday afternoon. We need proof of life.

The place looks like Cupid attacked it like Buddy the Elf. There are shimmering cellophane hearts hanging from the ceiling and pink strands of tinsel dangling dangerously close to the open flame of a champagne-scented candle. I make a sharp left at the *actual* bow and arrow aimed at the cereal aisle. At least someone thought to stick a jumbo marshmallow on the tip. Safety first.

Coralee points at the open jar of pigs' feet dyed cotton-candy pink. "The FDA would not approve."

Bert is nowhere to be seen, but we do track down his mom in the back office. She's bobbing her head to something on her earbuds while staring at a spreadsheet that stretches across two different computer monitors. This is where Bert gets it.

"Hi, girls!" She beams when she sees us. Clearly, Bert did not tell her anything about what happened by the dumpsters. I stare at my red Converse—the only nod to V-Day I am willing to give.

Coralee speaks for us both. "Hiya, Mrs. Akers. We were just looking for Bert."

Her face falls. "Oh. He's at home. Resting. He's been under the weather the past few days."

"Well, tell him we hope he feels better real soon," Coralee says, and waves me out before I can quiz Mrs. Akers like I want to.

"What are you doing? We only know where he is, but we still have no idea *how* he is."

"Exactly. And you think he's going to tell his dear old mom any of that? If we want the real lowdown on Bert, we are going to have to shake it out of him ourselves." She takes a handful of conversation hearts from the basket by the cash register and tosses me one. It reads CUTIE PIE. She winks. "For your lover boy." I throw it at her head.

Later that night, I am feet up on the wall in the sewing corner, staring at the stupid candy heart that Coralee forced me to take back. I wonder if they make one that says SORRY I DESERTED YOU IN YOUR TIME OF NEED. Probably not. I should hire one of those skywriters to fly over his house and paint the air with smoky apology curlicues. Or I could just suck it up and say it myself. I pop the candy into my mouth and then spit it out again. Ick. Does anyone actually eat these?

When I was little and still in speech therapy, we used conversation hearts to work on my sounds and letters. The therapist had a whole bag made special with individual letters and also sign language. I made Mom a Valentine's Day card that spelled out my name and "I love you" in ASL. It was pinned on our fridge for years.

If I want to really prove to Bert that I'm sorry and yank him out of his funk, I'm going to have to pull out all the stops. I need something epic—something (and I can't even believe I'm thinking this) bigger than baked goods. It has to be something that says *You are my absolute best friend and together we* will *get you that scholarship.*

I sit up and scramble for my phone. The idea comes to me almost fully formed and ready to go, like those cooking videos where they show the mixing of ingredients and then cut to the steaming scones coming out of the oven.

It's almost midnight when I'm done planning it all out, but when I text Coralee, the bubbles of her reply appear immediately.

I'm innnnnnnnnnnnnnnnnnnnnnnn! she types. I can almost hear her cheering from the trailer next door.

It is the perfect plan. Now all I have to do is get him out of his house.

"You said Ellie was stuck in a ditch," Bert says to Coralee when she answers my door the following morning. She is outfitted in her silver puffer, earmuffs, and hiking boots so big, they have to be hand-me-downs of Dane's.

"Happy Valentine's Day!" I wave at him from behind her. "There's no ditch."

He starts to turn, but Coralee drags him in by his scarf and shuts the door.

"You hate Valentine's Day."

"I sure do." I grin at him.

He frowns. "So—"

"So we're taking back the holiday! Just like we did two years ago when we went miniature golfing."

He sticks his hands in his pockets. "I don't want to play mini golf." Wow, pouting Bert. He really does look his age. "Oh, you have plans? Going to the dance with Sierra tonight after all?"

He tilts his head. "Sierra? Why would I go to a dance with Sierra?"

My smile gets a teensy bit wider. She's not even on his radar. I don't even think he knew she was asking him out after assembly.

"Well, we aren't playing golf. It's something better. I promise." I wheel toward him. I am sweating in my fleece jacket and the sequined purple scarf Coralee added for "charm and sparkle." We are all set to go. Except, if he says no, it was all for nothing. A plan is only perfect if you get everyone to participate.

I don't deserve a second chance, but I put my mittened hands together anyway. "Bert, I'm sorry. I was a terrible friend. I'm sorry I stopped helping you with the scholarship, but please let me make it up to you. Please?"

He looks at me, *really* looks at me, and then nods, his red hat bobbing. "Okay." He does not smile, but it's enough.

"Ooooo-kay!" Coralee sings, and takes a running punch at his arm. She hits when she's mad and she hits when she's glad. Coralee is a hazard in any mood.

Brilliant cold sunlight streams in the door when we throw it open. It is absolutely freezing and absolutely gorgeous. The perfect weather for an adventure.

Hutch comes down the hallway from the kitchen with

a dish towel over his shoulder. "Where're you kids off to?" He is attempting to make Mom a special Valentine's lunch. So far he has burned three heart-shaped grilled cheese sandwiches, but I am saying nothing.

"Susie's shuttling us to the mall for V-Day makeovers," Coralee replies, batting her eyelashes at him. "In fact"—she points at him with her hot-pink nail—"a little bronzer would make those cheekbones pop. Wanna come?"

He holds up his spatula. "I got enough on my plate here. You kids have fun. Ellie"—he turns to me—"take an extra jacket just in case."

"Thanks, but nope." I hurry out the door. I listen to Hutch when he tells me how many reps of free weights I should do. But I do not have to listen to him when he tells me how to dress.

"Take a right, people!" I order as soon as we're free. Coralee and Bert follow me around the corner of the house, down the concrete path, past the garden, and into the woods. Above us the only birds in the bare trees are crows. They watch us with their beady eyes. I shiver. It's much colder under the shadow of the trees.

"We are currently heading northeast," Bert says without consulting a map, because he is a walking compass. "The highway runs northwest and the town is south." He stops. "You are literally taking us nowhere."

"Are you going to complain this whole time?" I stop to look at him—secretly grateful to give my arms a rest from the bumpy forest path. "Because that's not the Bert I know."

"She's right," Coralee adds. "The Bert we know sees an obstacle and then, after analyzing it for a thousand years, conquers it. He powers through!"

Bert studies his boots. "Not anymore." He looks small. He sounds lost.

"Bert," I say. "I promise this is a good surprise. Ten more minutes and then you'll find out. I swear."

We start moving again. And for the remainder of the time, there is nothing but the sound of leaves crunching and the puff of our breath throwing white clouds in the air.

Almost exactly ten minutes later, the trees open up and we reach a fence. It borders a large pasture filled with cows. Coralee props one foot up on the lowest rail and shouts, "Ta-da!"

Bert looks at her, then the fence, then the cattle, then at me.

"It's a dead end."

"Incorrect, sir! It is a beginning!" I clap my hands together, because I'm trying to hype up the moment and also because I'm freezing. "Today you have an opportunity to go above and beyond. Today, my dear Bert, is the day you prove to Brighton Academy that you are worthy of their attention and—"

"Money!" Coralee shouts.

"I was going to say 'respect.'"

"That too."

"I'm not applying." He looks straight at me. "You were right to quit. The odds were not in my favor. I wasn't going to get in."

My heart double-beats. He thinks I quit because I didn't think he'd get the scholarship. He has *no idea* it's because I thought he would. I smile through the hiccup in my throat.

"Oh, Berto, you better listen up. You *will* get in, and *this* is how you're going to do it." I point to the pasture.

He stares at the cows. They ignore us—black blobs in a sea of dead grass. I'll admit, it's a little anticlimactic.

"Not them." I roll over to him, reach up, and turn his head toward the left. His cheeks are cold through my mittens. "*That.*"

Several yards away, a metal gate with a rusted latch breaks up the mile-long stretch of fencing that separates the pasture from the forest. I found this spot last summer on one of my long fitness rolls.

"Today, Bert, *we* are going silvopasturing," I tell him.

His head whips around so fast under my hands that I accidentally smack him.

"What do you mean 'going' silvopasturing? That is not a thing."

Coralee hops down from her perch on the highest rail and slaps him on the back. "It is today, my friend. Ellie, get your phone ready. We need to document this."

"For research," I tell him. I pull out my phone and announce into the camera, "Today we are releasing these cows into the wild so that cattle plus forest plus crop can intermingle like God intended."

I call over my shoulder, "Coralee, gate."

She runs over to the gate. It has a lock that I know for a fact is rusted through. She studies it, takes a few steps back, then takes a flying leap, kicking it as hard as she can. It clangs loudly but doesn't budge while she bounces back like a pinball. A few cows glance over, their huge brown eyes sleepy and bored.

"Aaaaannnd cut," I say, pocketing my phone and rolling to the gate. I take off my mitten and with two fingers lift the lock off its metal chain. It wasn't even closed. I toss it to Coralee.

"*Now* get the gate."

"Show-off," she says.

When she swings it wide, I turn to Bert. "All right, buddy, time to shine."

He leans against the fence and crosses his arms.

"Seriously," I say. "Get going."

"This is not how silvopasturing works. It is a precise incorporation of farmland, livestock, and forest. It takes years to establish. You can't just throw open a gate!"

Now it's my turn to cross my arms. This is getting ridiculous. I know I'm supposed to stay humble or whatever like Mema said, but here I am doing all I can to make things right and he won't even give it a *try*.

"You want to stay here and pout? Fine! We're going without you. Aren't we, Coralee?"

"You bet your bottom dollar we are!"

"Did I remember to tell him whose land this is, Coralee?"

"You did not."

We smile at each other. If this doesn't get him moving, nothing will.

"Cole's daddy," Coralee says, beating me to it.

"If this works," I add, "poor Cole's going to have a whole lot of work ahead of him, rounding up these cows."

I don't wait for Bert to answer. Coralee is off at a dead sprint, and I'm right behind her. He can follow or not.

"Yeehaw!" Coralee shouts.

"Giddyup!" I call as we race toward the cows like our lives depend on it.

We get closer and closer and they get bigger and bigger and then, instead of scattering like birds the way I expected, they just . . . stand there. I hit the brakes one foot from the nearest hoof.

"Come on! Move it or lose it!" Coralee claps. She stomps. She marches in a circle around them. Nothing. After she's worn herself out, she comes panting over to me. Bert ambles up nice and slow on my right. But he's here.

"Maybe we need to scare them?" I ask him. He shrugs. I shout, "Boo!" One of them poops. None of them move.

Coralee flops down in the grass. Bert begins to make a wheezing sound. I look over to check on him. It's not wheezing. He's laughing!

I throw my mitten at him. "I don't see you doing any better!"

He squats down next to me so we are watching the cows together. He takes off his hat and rests his elbows on his knees.

"You look like a good old-fashioned cowboy," I tell him. "Maybe *you* can be the cow whisperer."

"Did you know that some farmers use music to increase the milk production of their cattle?" he asks.

"Did you know that I do not spend my free time reading about milk production?"

Bert has done nothing but complain, but now he's

smiling when he looks at me, and dang, it's good to see him excited about some factoid again.

"It's true. Cows are highly susceptible to music. It's a proven stress reliever."

"Grandpa Dane plays bluegrass for the cockatoos, and it puts them right to sleep," Coralee adds from my other side. "He says music soothes the savage beast. Hasn't had much of an effect on Bunny, though."

"We don't want to put them to sleep. We want to get them moving!" I shout, extra loud—not one stinking tail-swish for my effort.

"You have to choose the right song," Bert says.

"You got anything in mind?" What kind of mood-boosting playlist do you make for a cow?

Coralee snaps her fingers. Bert and I watch as she fishes her phone out of her Levi's and begins to scroll. "E, start recording. This is *the one*, people."

I zoom in on Coralee, her blond hair blowing in the winter wind. She smiles her beauty-pageant smile and hits play.

A piano and a guitar burst through the tiny speaker at high volume. The cows look up. All of them.

"Uh, Coralee—"

She turns the volume up louder. The cows start to moan and shift.

Dolly Parton's voice rings out over their lowing. She's singing "Nine to Five" and Coralee is so busy tapping out the rhythm with her too-big shoe that she doesn't notice the panicked look in the whites of the cows' eyes. But I do. And so does Bert.

He gets to his feet slowly. I start to roll backward.

"Coralee," I whisper. She can't hear me. "Coralee!" I shout just as a cymbal crashes over the airwaves. The cows *lose* it. They take off running. Straight. At. Us.

Coralee drops the phone and runs. I'm bumping over clumps of grass and dirt so fast my teeth are knocking together and my arms are screaming. We are so close! The gate is yards and then feet away and then I am through, with Bert just behind.

I wheel around. Coralee is dead even with the lead cow. It's a race to the finish line, and I can see the panic in both their eyes.

"Runnnn!" I scream just as she hurls herself past me. Bert slams the gate shut. The cows pull up short, their hot breath steaming up the air and bits of saliva dripping along the fence rail.

"Well, I guess we know what gets them moving," I say as Coralee collapses flat on the ground and Bert bends over with his hands on his knees.

"If anyone could, it's Dolly," Coralee says to the sky.

I turn to Bert. "Sorry about the failed experiment."

He straightens up and stretches his back. "Not a failure. We got some excellent data points to add to my application."

"Your . . . application? So you're *not* quitting?"

He looks at me and smiles. "I'm just sorry Cole doesn't have to catch his cows."

Coralee kicks the fence with her boot. "There's still time. Round two?"

Bert and I shake our heads and then start laughing, because holy Moses, we just got chased by cows!

"I'm glad y'all think this is funny," Coralee says, still flat on the ground. "Who's going back to get my phone?"

15

The Waiting Game

The calendar says it's still winter, but nature does not agree. The crabapples have budded, and the squirrels are louder than ever on the tin roof. They sound like they've taken up Zumba.

I throw a balled-up sock at Bert. He catches it one-handed without looking. We are in the sewing corner with our legs up on the wall, and he has been staring at the last sentence of his scholarship essay for *ten* minutes.

"If you don't hurry up and hand that over, I am leaving you here to rot. We can use your decaying body to mulch Mema's flower bed."

He taps away at his laptop. Delete-delete-delete. Then he types some more and deletes again. I grab his hand.

"You're going in the wrong direction, Bert."

He lets his head fall back and surrenders the laptop. "It's the first week of March. The application is due in nine days. I'll never finish."

"Of course you will. You've filled out all the forms. Your digital model of the silvopasture is amazing. Now all you have to do is finish this essay."

He rubs his eyes and mutters, "All I have to do. Like it's easy."

"It is! You just have to explain why protecting the environment is important to you."

I read his essay again for the twelfth time. It's good. The grammar is correct. The thesis tracks all the way to the end, but . . .

"The facts are in place. Now you have to *show* them why it's important to you."

"The facts speak for themselves."

"In this case, Bert, I think you need to speak for *yourself*."

He thumps the back of his head against the floor. "I don't know how."

"Sure you do. You just need to add a little more emotion. Show them what it would mean to finally be in a place with people who understand you."

"You understand me."

Above us, the squirrels start to tango, and my heart picks up the beat. I study him out of the corner of my eye. The tips of his ears look pink. It's probably just the heat. We're right next to the vent.

"I mean your fellow science nerds."

He looks at his feet. His socks have bald eagles on them. Another gift from his sister. "Right."

"And tell them what you would do with all the resources at your fingertips, like the greenhouse and the big fancy labs that we don't have at Lakeview."

"I'm not good with words. I should just get you to write it for me."

I push the computer over to him. "It's almost there. One more revision and you're done. Next stop, Brighton."

The name of the school plops between us, a sticky glob of conflict I can't look at, but that doesn't matter. What matters is that I am helping Bert again. I never should have quit in the first place. You don't quit your friends—even when you wish they were more than that.

But that doesn't make this any easier. He's so close that when he shifts, his elbow just barely touches my upper arm. He doesn't move it. My arm is electric. It could power all the Wi-Fi from here to Utah. The fish-swishy feeling hits me like a wave.

I sit up fast enough to get dizzy.

"You want a snack? Popcorn? Homemade Cheez-Its? Raisinets?" Seriously, Raisinets? Am I eighty?

Before he can choose, my phone buzzes in my pocket. It's Mema, which is weird, since she never dials my cell. She always calls the ancient landline in the kitchen, with its twenty-foot cord that catches on my wheelchair handle every time I roll by.

"Hey, Mema."

"Who is this?" an angry voice shouts from the other end.

"Grandpa?"

"Marianne, that you?"

"Grandpa, it's me, Ellie!" Why does he have Mema's phone? Where *is* Mema? What's going on?

"You stole my boat! I told—" The line goes staticky for a second and his voice drops out. I hit speakerphone and Bert leans in. "Thieves, all of them!" he finishes. Before I can ask him to repeat himself, a whooshing sound like running water or wind fills the still, hot air of my bedroom.

"Grandpa, are you outside?" I drop the phone and scramble to get my chair. Bert picks it up and hands it back to me once I'm situated.

"I'm in the lake and there's no boat! Where's my boat?" This time I can clearly hear the sound of splashing, like he's *in* Lake Eufaula right this minute. The phone cuts out again.

"Grandpa!" I scream. Fear rises up in me like a wild animal. Bert runs for the door.

"Who is this?" Grandpa asks again in a voice grown quiet with panic.

"It's me, Grandpa! It's Ellie! Your granddaughter!" I yell, because my panic makes me louder.

"Who?"

I start to cry.

Seconds later, Bert rushes back into my room with Mom and Hutch. Mom grabs the phone from me. "Dad, it's me. Stay on the line, okay? Someone is coming to get you. Just stay on the line."

Mema sits sandwiched between Mom and Hutch. She is in pajamas and her pink zippered housecoat. Her hair is wet. She was taking a shower when Grandpa wandered out this afternoon. The home nurse, not Anvi but another one, had gotten up to use the restroom. It wasn't long, a couple of minutes maybe, but that was all it took. Grandpa walked right out the patio doors with Mema's phone and waded straight into the pond. He thought it was Lake Eufaula. He was planning on fishing. He went to look for his boat. At least that's what he told the emergency responders who wrapped him in thermal blankets and took him to the hospital for monitoring.

I can just see him wandering into the pond, icy water sloshing up into his sneakers and then crawling up the legs of his pants until he is stiff and lost and turning circles in a body of water that is not what he thought. I squeeze my eyes shut to chase away the image, but that only makes it sharper, so I open them and study the dull waiting-room walls.

I have never been to this hospital before. It is much smaller and older than where Dr. Hirschman has his office. The waiting room smells like dust and Clorox. The chairs are thin plastic instead of fabric. There is only one small window. It overlooks a Hardee's across the street.

I rock back and forth at the end of our row. I want to get closer to Mema, but I can't. I wish I were little and could sit in her lap. I wish it was like it used to be when we'd visit from Nashville and she would make Grandpa sleep on the couch so I could stay in her bed with her and fall asleep holding her hand.

She coughs and Mom leans into her. Hutch reaches across the back of his seat so he can wrap his arm around them both. Suddenly, they are a circle and I am on the outside and I don't know how to break in. I roll to the window and message Bert and Coralee.

I text, still waiting

Coralee sends ten thumbs-down emojis and then a fist and a heart.

Bert's bubbles appear and then disappear without a response. My heart dips. I put my phone away. He said he wasn't good with words.

Eventually, when the brightest thing in the sky is the red Hardee's sign, a doctor comes out and stops in front of Mema.

"Mrs. Cowan?"

Mema jerks like she was asleep, but she wasn't. "That's me."

The doctor, a kind-faced woman with cropped gray hair, shakes Mema's hand and then Mom's and Hutch's and then she holds her hand out to me, too. We shake. She gives a little squeeze at the end. I can't tell if that's good or bad.

"Mr. Cowan has been moved from the ER to a patient room. He is on oxygen but he's stable. But we'd like to keep him for monitoring. His body temperature and blood pressure were quite low when he came in, and we want to make sure he's stable and safe to come home."

I'm still sifting through the mess of good and less good news in all those words when Mema pushes herself up on unsteady legs.

"I want to see him."

"It's probably best to let him rest for now."

Mema crosses her arms over her housecoat. "I know what's best."

"Mom," my mom says, and reaches up to touch her elbow. I hold my breath. For once I don't know who to root for.

"Jonah and I have never spent a night away from each other in the last sixty years. We are not starting now." She turns to Mom. "You go on home. I'll call you in the morning."

"Marianne—" Hutch begins.

"No. I appreciate you all being here, but I need time with my husband." She looks at me. "Ellie, you take care of your mama for me, all right?"

"Yes, ma'am." I nod, relieved to have a job.

Mom starts to argue, but the line of Mema's mouth is set. She's made up her mind, and there's nothing the doctor or anyone else can do about it.

16
On the Mend

We drive home with the radio on low volume. It's set to a country station nobody likes, but none of us has the energy to change it. I am in my blue flannel pajamas and lighting my candle in the Serenity Palace when Mom knocks on the door.

"Hey, kiddo. You all settled? It's time for bed." She talks to me like I am six again and need her help with the toilet and my chair. I thought I was supposed to be taking care of *her* for once.

"I'm not tired," I say, which is a lie. "And I promised I'd call Coralee when I got home." Not a lie.

"Honey, it's late. And you've got school in the morning."

"I'm not going to school. I'm going with you to the hospital tomorrow."

She comes in and closes the door behind her. My spacious spa feels not so spacious anymore.

"No, you're not. We don't even know if Grandpa can have any visitors."

"They let Mema stay."

Mom sighs and leans against the counter. "That's because she's too hardheaded to do any different."

I cross my arms. "So am I. I'm going."

"Ellie, can you not fight me on every little thing!"

"I'm not!" My voice almost breaks on "not." I will not cry. I chase away the sadness with what I've wanted to say for months. "I just want to see him before you send him back to the old folks' home that let him wander off by himself in the *first place*."

"Do not start with this," Mom warns. Hutch raps on the door.

"Everything okay in here?"

"No," I say exactly as Mom says, "Yes."

Hutch cracks open the door. Because I am a logical human making a logical argument, I hold my voice steady when I say to both of them, "He'd be much better off here than in a place like that."

Mom narrows her eyes. "What do you mean, 'here'?

As in here in this trailer? Ellie, we tried that, remember? It's why we moved to Eufaula to begin with, but it didn't work out. He needs to be at Autumn Leaves."

I throw my hands up and the candle sputters out. "Clearly, he doesn't! If they can't keep him safe there, why can't we try again here? Why can't you trust that someone else other than *you* might know better?"

"Your grandfather's health is a risk I'm not willing to take! We know the chronological progression of the disease. It doesn't get better. Moving home isn't going to fix him!"

The room blurs before I can blink fast enough to chase back the tears. I'm glad the candle's out. It's easier to hide hurt in the dark. She doesn't get it. I don't want to fix him. I just miss him! She never lets me get all the way to the end of what *I* need to say before she states her own opinion as fact.

I'm about to tell her this, if I can get my throat unclogged enough to speak, but Hutch breaks in first. "Ellie, your mother has a point. Jonah is—"

I smack the counter. The sting of it clears both my tears and my throat. "Of course you're going to agree with her. That's all you ever do! I liked you better before you married my mom." Hutch takes a step back from the doorway.

"Ellie! Go to your room!" Mom shouts.

"Fine! Get out of my way, then!"

When she moves enough that I can squeeze my chair by, I roll down the hallway past them both and slam the door. I feel the force of it all the way up my arm and into my heart. I'm not sorry. I'm not.

Light falls meanly across my eyes way too early the next morning. My whole body aches from the tension of yesterday. All I want to do is pull the covers over my head and sleep until summer. But my phone is buzzing on the nightstand, and if I don't pick it up, I know I will have a blond-haired triple threat climbing through my window any minute.

"Sorry I didn't call last night," I mumble into the phone.

"I didn't know to expect a call."

I sit up and rub my eyes. It's Bert, not Coralee.

"Oh, hi."

"Hi," he says.

"Hi," I say again because my brain is short-circuiting. Bert never calls. He says he's not a "phone person."

"I've been reading up on prognoses of people who have had an experience similar to your grandfather's."

"Are there a lot of people wandering into ponds that I don't know about?"

"Well, the conditions weren't exact, but it appears the outcome looks good based on how quickly he received aid."

"Thanks, Bert." I smile into the phone.

"Of course. I just thought you would like to know."

"That was very thoughtful."

"And I'll collect your assignments today. I'm assuming you're not coming to school."

I glance at the clock. It's after when we usually leave, but last night Mom said I had to go.

"Umm, I'm not sure yet. I'll text you. Okay?"

"All right," he says, and hangs up before I have a chance to say bye.

When I roll into the kitchen, Mom is dumping the last of her coffee down the sink. She's dressed, but in an old University of Oklahoma sweatshirt of Hutch's, not her normal work clothes. Her back is to me, so she jumps when I ask, "Are you off to the hospital now?"

She turns. "*We* are off to the hospital. All three of us. I called Susie and asked her to drive Coralee and Bert to school."

That must be why Coralee wasn't shimmying through my window at daybreak. Before I can thank her, Hutch comes in the back door, rubbing his hands together and blowing on them. The hint of spring we had yesterday must have disappeared again. I can hear the wind rattling the windows. "Started the van for us. It'll be a minute before it warms up, though."

He smiles in my general direction but does not look at me.

"Thanks," I mumble while my face gets hot with shame. He nods.

Mom looks from him to me. "Go throw some clothes on and we'll head out, all right?"

I'm ten hours late on an apology to him. Now I don't know how to start. I mean, this is *Hutch*—the guy who built me my very own Serenity Palace and started the roller derby specifically so I could have something to look forward to in gym. He's made my mom happier than she has ever been. And I basically told him we were better off without him. The weight of my own words makes me sag in my chair. I don't even know how to begin to make up for it, so I roll back down the hall to get changed and don't say anything at all.

The hospital is hoppin' this morning. Orderlies zip past with trays of Jell-O and mini muffins and soupy-looking scrambled eggs. I remember these meals from all my previous stays. They are the same in every hospital. Applesauce that's the same temperature as the mashed potatoes, and ice cream so hard from being refrozen you have to chew it.

The receptionist directs us to the second floor, where we make a left past the coffee station and stop at room 205. A corner room. Everyone knows that's prime real estate in the hospital world—more windows, bigger bathroom, less foot traffic. The door is open as we approach. Another good sign. The serious cases are closed-door only.

I wheel with one hand and hold the tin of mini lemon tarts on my lap with the other. I didn't have time to make anything new, and I had these in the freezer from a test batch for the pie bake-off. Grandpa loves fruity desserts the best. Hopefully these will do.

I stop right before the door. Mom and Hutch are behind me, so they stop too. The rest of the world keeps moving. A nurse hurries by, her rubber clogs squeaking on the floor. A pack of doctors move from one room to the next, clicking their pens and tapping on iPads. All around us machines wheeze and beep, doing whatever they do to get everyone healthy and out the door.

Fear keeps its hand on the brakes. This is ridiculous! Grandpa is fine! They wouldn't put him in a regular room and let him have visitors if he wasn't. *Suck it up, Ellie. Get a move on.* But I can't make my arms do the necessary motions to wheel me through the door.

Hospitals save lives. They've saved mine. But the truth is, I hate them. Because they are also where people go when they can't be saved.

Mom puts a hand on my shoulder. "We'll do it together." She looks at Hutch. He pulls off his baseball cap like he's about to enter church.

"Okay," I say.

"Okay," Mom says.

We all file in all at once.

The room is empty.

"What in the world?" Mom turns a full circle, like Grandpa might be hiding under the tiny sink.

"Did we get the wrong room?" Hutch steps out to check the number again.

But I see *Jonah Cowan* scrawled across the whiteboard with his oxygen levels, his nurse's name, Micky, and what he ate for breakfast—Cream of Wheat and orange juice.

"Maybe Mema kidnapped him and they made a run for it."

But before Mom can say, *Don't joke, Ellie*, a nurse backs into the room, pulling a rolling oxygen tank, with Grandpa and Mema right behind him.

"Well, hello, Cowan family!" The nurse's arm muscles pulse as he slaps sanitizer on his hands. When his navy-blue scrub top stretches tight, I spot a tattoo of an anchor on his bicep. He could give Hutch a run for his money. "Jonah here just took three laps around the floor without stopping!"

While Micky helps Grandpa back into bed, his thin hospital gown fluttering around his shins like a dress, Mema beams like he finished a marathon. Grandpa's face is pale and shiny, though. I set the tin of lemon tarts on the edge of the bed.

"Hey, Grandpa," I say when Mom finally finishes her too-long hug.

"Hey, kiddo," he wheezes. The oxygen tubes dangling from his nose look like walrus whiskers. It'd be funny on any other day in any other place. "You bring me something sweet—other than you?"

Micky laughs like it's the best joke he's heard all year.

"Mini tarts. They're lemon."

"My favorite!" They aren't his favorite. I know this. He says that about everything I make, which makes me smile for real. My shoulders relax. Maybe he really is okay.

He fumbles with the lid. I help him pop it open and pass them around to everyone, including Micky, who takes one before he leaves to check on his other patients.

"They're weaning him off the oxygen." Mema smooths Grandpa's hair down where it stands straight up on one side. "If all goes well, he'll be leaving tomorrow." She squeezes his arm. She's wearing her favorite gray sweatshirt with the candy canes that she stitched herself. Mom must have come back last night to drop some things off for her. I wonder how long she stayed. I wonder what she and Mema talked about.

When Mom and Hutch and Mema go out in the hall to talk to the doctor, I roll closer to Grandpa's bed. It's not as close as I'd like, but it's the best I can do because of the safety rail.

"How you holding up?"

"That's what I'm supposed to ask you," I say.

"Pshaw." He swats at the thin, nubby blanket. "I'm tired of people fussing over me. Tell me something good."

I hunt around in my brain for a safe zone, something that won't make him confused or angry or . . . not himself.

"I'm starting to test out more recipes for the pie bake-off."

"The one at the fish fry in May?"

I nod so hard I rattle my chair. He remembers the fish fry and when it is!

"Yeah, but I still don't know what to do. It's got to be a showstopper, something no one's done before. If I see another chocolate chess pie, I'm going to flip the tent."

Grandpa lets out a wheezy laugh. I fight the urge to tell

him to take it easy. I don't want to be one of those people who make a fuss.

"You'll figure it out. You always do. Now listen, Ellie girl." He squints over at the door. "I got to say something before the cavalry comes back in."

"Uh, all right."

"Something that's just between you and me—" He grabs for my hand with icy fingers. A shiver of worry runs through me, but I hold still. He whispers something I don't catch at first.

"What, Grandpa?"

I lean in closer.

"I said *you* are my favorite granddaughter," and then he laughs again, louder this time—no wheezing involved.

"I'm your *only* granddaughter." I pretend to roll my eyes, but inside I'm a Zumba-dancing squirrel. He made a bad joke! You can't make bad jokes when you're sick!

"I mean it. You have always been mighty." He pats my hand, scattering little bits of pie crust on the bedsheet. "Maybe it's because you had to be from the beginning, but I'm gonna steal some credit. Those freckles"—he touches my nose—"aren't the only thing I gave you. We Cowans are tough cookies."

"Thanks, Grandpa." I squeeze his hand.

He winks and lays his head back.

I scoot away from the bed to let him rest and pop a small wheelie, like a silent cheer. Grandpa is on the mend *and* I got to miss half a day of school. This is the worst-turned-best day of my life. Bert even braved an actual phone conversation to make sure I was okay. That's a sign from the universe. I have to tell him how I feel. I have to! It doesn't even matter that he probably doesn't like me back, because saying it is the mightiest thing to do.

"Love you, my girl," Grandpa calls when I am almost to the door.

"Love you back!" I shout, and then zigzag down the hall just to annoy Mom, because what is the point of life if you can't drive your mother crazy?

17

Say It Again, but This Time with Feeling

Dear David Lebovitz,

Please don't take this the wrong way, but I never thought I'd make one of your recipes. Not because they aren't all amazing and wonderful. It's because you live in France and put absinthe in ice cream and make very fancy things like cherry clafoutis (which I had to check the spelling of three times). I'm just not sure my crowd would appreciate your particular tastes.

However, I am writing to take it all

back. Today I made your sablés Bretons, those crisp salted butter cookies, and they are incredible! I am now Team Lebovitz all the way! Vive la France! I followed your suggestion and used the highest quality salted butter in all of Oklahoma, or at least in the town of Eufaula, where I live. Our local Food & Co. stocks butter made from the milk of cows right here in our area. It better be the best butter, because our cows are super-high maintenance. (Don't ask me how I know that.)

Anyway, I made the cookies even though I thought there was way, way, way too much butter and not nearly enough of anything else in them. David, I was so wrong. They are melt-in-your-mouth fantastic. The person I want to share them with is a die-hard chocolate fan, but I'm hoping these will help him think outside the box a little about what he likes in food ... and people.

So, good job on the butter cookies and the whole living-in-France-when-you-are-not-French thing! Also, I am taking your suggestion and packing a thermos of coffee to go alongside the treats.

Your French convert,
Ellie

I'm not stalling. I'm really not. I was going to tell Bert right away yesterday when I got to school. The day got away from me, what with all the teachers asking about Grandpa while also piling on the homework. Then Coralee needed help rescuing Daisy from Bunny, who cornered her under the trailer. We had to coax them both out with chunks of ground round.

And then, I mean, I had to get the special butter and the cookies had to chill or they would spread like little sad pancakes. I cannot declare my feelings for Bert over sad pancakes.

But now it's a Saturday and I'm out of items on my to-do list and all that's left is to wait for Bert to show up and keep myself from hiding under this porch. I check my phone. Bert is due at eleven. Two minutes. Bert is never late. I fidget in my chair. I straighten Mema's white-and-blue-checkered tablecloth, which I spread over the glass table. I tighten the lid on the thermos of coffee so it stays hot. That eats up about four seconds.

We could do this inside. We have the place all to

ourselves. Mom and Hutch went to meet Mema at the hospital to pick up Grandpa. They are all coming back here for a late lunch before Mema and Grandpa have to return to Autumn Leaves. We are having a family meeting to discuss next steps. Fingers crossed the next step is moving them out of that place permanently. I have a good feeling about it! Wish I could say the same about what's getting ready to go down over here.

The breeze is chilly, but not brutal. It's first-toe-dip-in-the-pool cold, the kind you know you'll get used to. The trees that had buds last week have begun to open. Tiny white and pink flowers poke through. It sets a nice vibe.

I am readjusting the plate of cookies a quarter turn to the left when Bert rounds the corner. He is exactly on time. His jacket is open, and he wears a shirt with green stripes that I've never seen before. My heart thrums so fast I feel it in my throat. I shouldn't have had three cups of coffee. I think I might pass out.

"I made cookies!" I yell before he gets up the steps.

He grins and I cannot look at him. Instead, when he sits next to me on the rocking couch, I set the entire plate of cookies in his lap.

"Oh, thank you. Maybe just one for—" he begins. I

reach too fast for the thermos of coffee, and the couch starts rocking and half the cookies slide onto the ground.

He bends over and picks up every single crumb. He sets them in a neat pile on the table. I wish I were a turtle and my chair were a shell I could disappear into.

He examines the spread. Takes a sip of the extra-bold-blend coffee. "This is a lovely celebration." He thinks he is here to celebrate the fact that he turned in his scholarship application.

"Yeah, uh, now all we do is wait, right?"

"Exactly one month. They promised to let all applicants, both those who are selected and those who are not, know by April fifteenth."

"You nervous?" I ask.

He selects a cookie and pauses, like he is running a system check, before answering, "There's no need to be. I will either get in or I won't. It's out of my hands." I nudge his knee with mine. He looks at me sideways. "Okay, a little." That makes two of us.

"You'll get in and you'll get a full ride." I watch him eat a butter cookie.

He chews slowly and his eyes go wide. "These are . . . extraordinary."

I grin and lean over to take one, setting us rocking

again. "I know you like chocolate best, but I thought you might like to try something *different*." Oh jeez, what a way to transition, Ellie.

He takes another one. Two robins bicker over something in the pine tree near the garage. I try to swallow but can't. I just want to get this over with and eat a cookie.

"Speaking of different. There've been a lot of changes lately. I've—" Something catches my eye, a movement in the hedge. A head appears, a very *blond* head, followed by the rest of a grinning Coralee. Luckily, Bert is so busy brushing crumbs off himself that he doesn't notice. I glare so hard at her I could burn a hole in the sun. She shoots me two thumbs-up and reverses back into the hedge like a gopher.

"It's the second law of thermodynamics."

I turn back to Bert, who seems to be talking to himself.

"Sir Isaac Newton," he adds.

"Sorry, what?" On a normal day I can usually follow the trail of Bert's thoughts. But this is not a normal day.

He puts down his coffee. "You mentioned change. Matter is always changing. It shifts and becomes something new all the time."

"Right." I pause to try and fold his words into my own thoughts. "So what I think we're *both* saying is that nothing stays the same."

"Exactly!" He grins. "You always get it."

That's my sign. This is it. I sit forward, focus on a crack in the brick to the left of his head, and blurt out, "I like you, Bert!"

I do not let my eyes drift. I focus on the crack. I begin to count, because counting is supposed to calm you down. I wish I could hide in the Serenity Palace. I wish I had something to do with my hands.

"I like you, too."

Say what? I forget the crack.

"No, Bert. I mean I *like you* like you."

"I like you, too," he says again without blinking.

"Bert, I'm going to need you to use more words now," *before I totally lose my mind.*

He sits back like he's settling in for a long chat. "I've known it for a while."

"You . . . have?"

"Yes. You're my pi."

"I'm your pie?" I flash back to Coralee's conversation heart.

"Pi, p-i. To calculate the circumference of a circle, you multiply two times pi, which is three point one four. Then multiply that by the radius. In this instance, you are the three point one four."

"O-kay?"

I sit back again, possibly *more* confused than when we began. I wanted to have a conversation about feelings. How did we end up doing math?

"You're the one element in the equation that doesn't change. You're the pi. Get it?" He leans forward and grabs my hands. I drop the cookie. I don't care. Because then he says, "You're my constant, Ellie. That's what I'm trying to say."

A smile that could break open the sky spreads across his face, and I don't even know what my face is doing because the fish-swishy feeling is so strong it's blinding. Bert has never held eye contact this long, *ever*. There are flecks of gold in the brown of his irises I never noticed before. So *this* is being in "like." The way Mom has Hutch and Mema has Grandpa, I have Bert. Bert is my person.

I'm about to tell him this when the van rolls down the drive, stirring up gravel and busting up the moment all in one go. We shoot to either end of the couch as Mom and Hutch get out.

I put my foot down to try to stop the couch rocking. Bert does too. It makes me burst into a fit of giggles. Act *normal*, Ellie.

"Where are Mema and Grandpa?" I call out between hiccup-y laughs.

Then I catch the look on Mom's face. Nothing could hollow her out like that except . . . It hits my stomach first, a hot churning that makes my mouth fill with spit. My brain catches up a second later. It's Grandpa.

18
Everything Changes

Dear Deb Perelman at smittenkitchen.com,

"I am writing to you with some sad news." That's how the pastor's letter began in our church newsletter. "Sad news," like the church softball game has been rained out. You don't start a letter about someone dying with "sad news." "Soul-shattering," "world-ending"—sure. Not "sad."

You might remember my grandpa, Jonas Cowan. I've mentioned him to you in previous letters. He's the one who loves your challah French toast so much. He was supposed to come home from the hospital this week. He was recovering from hypothermia. They said it was mild. They said all they had to do was wean him off the oxygen. But I guess his heart couldn't take it. I made him a welcome-back cherry pie he never got to eat.

People drop off lasagnas and casseroles, but they keep stacking up in the deep freeze because none of us can stomach all that food. Nothing sounds good. I look in the fridge and see peppers going moldy and milk souring, but I don't want to make anything out of them. I guess that's why I'm writing. When you are really broken up about "sad news," do you ever just not want to cook? Cooking has always been a comfort. But right now it hurts, like picking at a splinter, to think about making something when the one person I want to give it to isn't here.

Thank you for all of your wonderful recipes and for making my grandfather smile over your extra-fluffy challah

French toast on more than one occasion.
He would have called you a good egg.
All my best,
Ellie the non-baker

It is a Thursday at three p.m., but Bethlehem Methodist Church is packed. People spill out onto the covered walkway in the front. The white lilies in their giant vases give off a heavy, too-sweet smell that makes me want to puke. But I am in the front row, stuck out in the center of the aisle, so I cannot puke. Or maybe I should if it would get me out of here quicker. Anvi from Autumn Leaves is here. So are a few old co-workers from Grandpa's job at the air force base in Midwest City. Dad and Meg and my half brothers came in from Nashville, too. They sit in the pew behind us. The boys wear suits. For once they do not shove. I wish they would—it would make things more normal. Nothing about this is normal.

The tag in the back of my blue dress itches my neck. At least I didn't have to wear black. Mema insisted we all wear robin's-egg blue. Grandpa's favorite color. He said it was because it was the exact shade of Mema's eyes. I can't see her eyes now. They are aimed at her lap, where she holds one of Grandpa's handkerchiefs. It is beige and does not match, but I don't think she picked it for the color.

Up front, Pastor Clark stands next to a big posterboard picture of Grandpa set up on an easel. The easel is crooked. One leg is shorter than the other. In the picture, Grandpa is smiling in a charcoal suit and red tie. His hair still has some red in it and his cheeks are fuller. It isn't a recent pic. I stare at it for so long that the lines of his face grow hazy.

"Today we are gathered here to celebrate the life of Jonah Cowan," Pastor Clark begins. He's even older than Grandpa. It's not fair.

"Jonah was a spirited man who lived his life to the fullest. He loved his wife of sixty-two years, Marianne, and his daughter, Alice, and granddaughter, Ellie, with that same enthusiasm. He was a devoted member of this congregation, and I think we can all appreciate the friendly level of competition he brought to the bass-fishing tournament each year."

A few laughs echo through the space. How can they laugh when my grandfather's ashes are sitting in an urn six feet away? I begin to rock back and forth in my chair.

"As all of you know, our dear Jonah fought a tough battle with Alzheimer's over these last few years. He fought bravely and never lost hope or his faith, and for that we know he is in a better place."

Better place? I rock faster. Mom puts a hand on my arm.

"We are so glad he is finally at peace. He is home."

The sickly sweet scent of lilies is too much. The lights are too dim. Sweat drips down my collar. The picture of Grandpa stares out smiling but not seeing. I've got to get away.

I am down the aisle and out the door as Pastor Clark holds his gnarled old hands up in the closing prayer. I do not wait for the amen.

Mema finds me under an oak tree near the creek that winds just behind the church, next to our favorite picnic table. It's the one we always claim at the fish fry in May.

She sits next to me and doesn't say anything. Her face is blotchy. There are dry patches under her nose that look raw. Someone braided her hair for her today, but I don't know who. That was always Grandpa's job.

"You didn't stay for the end."

Mema shakes her head. "I had about enough for one day."

"Me too."

She puts the hand that's holding the handkerchief over mine. The sound of the church doors opening makes us look up. People start to file out. Mom and Hutch begin to make their way over to us.

"He's not in a better place," I say.

Mema doesn't speak for a long time. "Not better for us," she says eventually.

"Not better for anyone!" I thump my armrests over and over, hard enough to shake my whole chair. Mema lets me do it until I wear myself out.

"It's difficult to know what's better when you're swimming in the water instead of alongside it." She wipes her nose, turning the red even redder. "We're all just trying to stay afloat."

When Mom and Hutch catch up, we head to the van together, all five of us, because Mom cradles Grandpa's bronze urn in her arms. My grandparents are finally coming home to stay with us.

I got my wish. I just didn't want it like this.

I am in the shed, hiding out from visitors, when Bert stops by that afternoon. He is in his Sunday suit and his hair is combed like it used to be before he went to Brighton.

"I brought you flowers." He hands me sunflowers wrapped in cellophane. They are so bright they hurt my eyes. I set them down on the cinder block next to the punching bag.

I don't say anything. He keeps standing there, staring at me, waiting for . . . something. But I don't have anything to give him, not anymore. I just want him gone. After a while of standing and staring, he dusts off a spot along the wall and sits, his long legs sticking straight out. The sight of him makes the walls close in.

He clears his throat.

"There's more than one law of thermodynamics," he says. "The second law is that everything changes. The first law states that all matter is finite."

He looks at me for a response. I don't have anything to say.

"So, what that means, if you think of it in relation to humans, is that all the pieces of us are always here. They are simply shifting and changing at alternate rates."

"I think you should leave." I can't look at him.

"What?"

"I *said*, I think you should leave." I stare at my robin's-egg-blue lap and think, *I will never wear this dress again.*

"But—"

"I don't want to talk about the laws of thermodynamics! It doesn't make it any better to think of my grandfather floating around in the air." A sob creeps up my throat, tries to choke me. "What good is it if I can't hug him or laugh at his dumb jokes? I don't want bits and pieces of him! I want all of him *here*."

"I was just—"

"Get out, Bert."

I keep my eyes trained on my blue dress so I don't have to watch him leave.

19

Peach Season

The rest of March passes in a blur of too-sunny days. I watch from my window as the trees turn greener and the smoke from the neighbors' chimneys dwindles to nothing. Then April rushes in with downpour after downpour of thunderstorms. They turn the potholes to puddles. The gravel road out front is a muddy river I couldn't cross if I tried. It's a relief.

Mom makes me go to school. Hutch meets me in the shed and I box until the sweat stings my eyes and my arms hang heavy. The ache in my arms is the only thing that stops the pain in my brain and my heart. But it doesn't last. I miss Grandpa. I caught myself humming "train a-comin'" in the shower last week and cried so hard my tears and the water fell together down the drain.

And I miss Bert. He's here but he's not. He's near me in class, across from me at the lunch table, at my side in the van, but we don't talk. He watches me, his whole body radiating a kindness I can feel even though I won't meet his eye. Last week he elbowed a handful of the green spearmint candies from Food & Co. toward me at lunch. He knows they're my favorite. I wouldn't let myself touch them until he got up to leave. They are in a little teacup on my bedside table now. They make me happy and sad at the same time. I should throw them away, but I can't.

I spend most of my free time hiding at Coralee's. She plays me songs on her guitar, and I lie on her bed with Francis nibbling at my sleeves. He doesn't understand why I don't bring him food anymore. I can't bake. I haven't made one thing since those butter cookies on that day in March.

Mema has taken up the dinner prep. She simmers vats of vegetable soup we never get all the way through before she starts on another one. She also does all the laundry. In the afternoons, I usually find her out on the porch with the ironing board and a pile of clothes on the rocking couch. Whenever Mom begs her to take a break, she waves her off with something about "earning my keep" now that she lives with us. But I think it's because she can't stay still.

She and I are back to sharing a bedroom, like we used to when I'd visit. It's the same, but not. Grandpa isn't snoring on the couch in the living room. Hutch is drawing up the plans for another extension like we did with my Serenity Palace, but much bigger.

When he showed me the blueprints, he said, "It will have a bedroom, bath, and kitchenette if I can work it right with the foundation. It's called a mother-in-law suite." It should be comforting that there are enough people in the world moving their mothers-in-law in with them that they need a name for it. But it's not.

For now, Mema is with me, and I know I'm almost in high school, but I'm glad. One night last week, I reached for her hand in the dark. I wasn't sure she was still awake. Her breathing had been steady for a while, but she held on tight to my fingers. We didn't talk. But it was nice to hold on to someone and know they are thinking the same things you are.

I'm out in the shed throwing punches at the boxing bag by myself because Hutch has started spring football coaching again, and I hear someone calling my name. It's Bert. My heart tugs toward the sound of his voice. I keep punching until he is so close that if I hit the bag once more it will smack him in the face. I stop.

He's holding a big wooden crate and his shorts are too short, like he went through a growth spurt on the way over. His shirt is the same green one he was wearing when I told him I liked him and he said he liked me back and for that one minute everything was perfect, before it fell apart.

I peel off the gloves and study my cracked knuckles, because it's easier than studying him.

He sets the crate at my feet.

"We just got these in from Georgia. I guess they had an early spring."

I peer between the slats.

"You brought me peaches."

"I did."

"Why?"

He doesn't say anything for the longest time. He's always been big on pauses, but this one is a doozy, long enough that I look up to see if he is still there. He is and he shrugs and the familiar gesture makes me want to lean into him. I do the opposite and roll back until I bump against the canning shelves.

"I thought you might like to make something with them."

My face gets hot. Why can't he just get it? My heart's

not fit to care about anybody or anything anymore. It's all busted up and full of holes.

"I don't bake anymore."

"Not right now."

I shake my head hard enough to clear it and get the last words out.

"Not *ever*, Bert. I'm done."

"Well, they're here if you need them."

We are not talking about peaches anymore and we both know it.

"Okay, thanks."

He kicks the dirt along the edge of the shed, where grass won't grow. "I got into Brighton."

My busted-up, holey heart crumbles a bit more. I knew he'd get in. I told myself a hundred times over the last few weeks that it would be better this way. He'll be gone for real, so I can start forgetting him.

I wheel around so I am facing the back wall. "Congratulations," I mumble. "Thank you for the peaches." My pulse ticks double-time trying to keep my body still.

When I finally hear the sound of his footsteps crunching on gravel, I bend over and tuck my arms into my stomach, holding the pieces of myself together. I don't turn around until I know he's all the way gone. When I do, the peaches are still there, sitting in their box in a spot of sun.

I let the box sit at the edge of the canning shed for two full days until Mom finally picks it up and carries it onto the porch. The three of us, me, Mom, and Mema, take our places on the rocking couch with our elbows on our knees and stare at the peaches as if they hold the mysteries of the universe.

"Use it or lose it," Mema says.

"It's like riding a bike," Mom adds.

"You know those mean opposite things, right?" I say.

Mema points at the peaches. "Don't change the subject. It's time to put the gifts the good Lord gave you to use."

"I can't," I whine toward the peaches and the universe.

"Well, if you don't, I will." Mema gets up from the couch and disappears into the kitchen. She comes out a few minutes later with her favorite white-handled paring knife and a yellowing spiral cookbook. It's the *Bethlehem Methodist Ladies' Cookbook* from 1984. Her favorite.

She cuts into a peach and passes around slices. Then she opens the cookbook and flips to the index. "Hmmm, peach cobbler—well, we know you can already do that. Peach melba. I'm not even sure what that is."

"It's peaches in raspberry sauce with vanilla ice cream," I say because I can't help myself, and slurp a drip of peach juice from my wrist. It is sweet, but not as sweet as our Oklahoma variety. Prime peach season is July. This peach is good, but it's a shadow of the real thing.

"Peach parfait. Peach snickerdoodles. Peach tarts with pecans." Mema reads all the way down the list and then closes the book. My fingers itch to take it from her. They both look at me, waiting. My chest gets tight.

"The last thing I made was the day Grandpa died," I whisper, remembering the sablés Bretons that were supposed to change my life. "It hurts to think about trying again."

Mema puts a hand on my knee. "I know it does, baby girl. We weren't ever promised a life without hurt." A tear leaks down her cheek, traveling a winding path of wrinkles until it drips off her chin. "But that doesn't mean it can't still be sweet, too." She fishes a hanky out of her pocket. It's the same old beige one of Grandpa's.

When Mom begins to sniff, Mema sits up straight again, says, "That's enough of that," and hands me another peach along with her knife. I cut it into perfectly even slices. The motion feels good, like crying when you can finally get it out.

The next morning I am at Bert's door, holding the most perfect cinnamon streusel peach muffin the world has ever known. My pulse hammers so loud in my ears I can't even hear myself knock.

"You're right," I spit out before he can even say hello. He is still in his pajamas. It's adorable. "You're my pi, too. I'm sorry I pushed you away. Here." I shove the muffin at him like it's a live grenade. He cups it in his hands.

"Umm, okay?"

Interesting. Early-morning Bert is way less coherent than post-coffee Bert. I take advantage of his silence. I need to get this out.

"I still like you and I don't want to lose you." I take a deep breath. "But I'm going to anyway. You're leaving for Brighton this summer and there's nothing I can do about it. So we have to be rational, right?" I shift in my chair. "It makes the most sense to just stay friends and enjoy the time we have." There. Done. And my voice didn't shake once, even though my heart is poised on the edge of a cliff.

He scratches his head and picks at the muffin but does not taste it. I try to swallow but my whole body seems to have frozen now that the words are out.

"Well," he says after an eternity. "I think the most *rational* thing is to approach this like any experiment."

My heart stirs, even though I ordered it not to get its hopes up. "How do you mean?"

"I mean . . ." He pauses, bites into the muffin, and

chews at least five hundred times. Mema's favorite phrase, "slow as molasses," comes to mind while I wait for him to speak again. "We have formed a hypothesis, which is that we want to be in each other's lives as *more* than friends."

I nod.

"So, I guess the next step is to test it out and gather data. Then, after a prolonged period of time—I'd say at least six months—analyze and reevaluate."

"Six months, huh?"

"At the least."

He smiles. He sets the muffin down. Then he cups my face in his hands and kisses me. His lips taste like butter and cinnamon, and he smells like laundry right out of the dryer. I forget what words are.

It's only a few seconds, but when he pulls back, I have to stop myself from rolling forward.

"For data collection purposes," he says with a lopsided grin that makes my heart do a quick backflip and fall into the splits.

"Of course." I grin back. "It's only logical."

20

It's Not Goodbye, It's Jalapeño

Dear Grandpa,

I decided to write to you like I do all my favorite chefs. I hope that's okay. It's the best way I say what needs saying, second to baking, of course.

I want you to know that I miss you every day. Every second. I bet you do know that, because Mema says you're watching over us, making sure we aren't ruining your garden or messing with your tools. We aren't, I promise. But Hutch did fix your fishing boat, which is why we're going out on the lake today. It's for you.

You inspired my best bake yet, which means I am now the first-place blue-ribbon winner of the Bethlehem Methodist annual pie contest for the second time! I won, Grandpa, and it's because of you. I got to thinking about that story you told about how your peach tree wouldn't blossom when it was alone and how that's true of people, too. We need each other, whether we like it or not. So I made fried peach hand pies with a peach glaze and crystallized peach sugar on top. It was a peach extravaganza in your honor.

Grandpa, I promise to take care of your people—Mema and Mom and myself, too, as best I can. That's what you always did for us. Thank you for that. And thank you for giving me my freckles and making me mighty. Thank you for loving me.

Yours forever,
Ellie Cowan,
blue-ribbon baker extraordinaire

It's late July, and the waters are still when Hutch steers the boat out onto the lake. The sun has just begun to set, painting the waves lavender and pink. Coralee and Bert sit on the shore, waiting for our return. It's the magic hour, that wobbly time between afternoon and night that was always Grandpa's favorite. Mom and Mema hold hands when Hutch cuts the engine. I am in my water chair in the front. I look out toward the bright orange buoys bobbing under the bridge and hold on tight to Grandpa's urn, which is nestled in my lap.

At Mema's nod, I lift the lid and hold it out. We each take a small handful of ashes. I don't want to let go. I can hear Coralee strumming on her guitar. She's singing "Lean on Me" in her lowest, softest voice—the one she saves for midnight calls and gospel songs. I close my eyes against the wind and the sting of tears, and with Mom and Mema, I open my hand. Now a part of him is in the place he was happiest in the world.

When we get back to shore, Hutch hauls the boat up onto the sand so that I can transfer into my chair. He knows I like to do it myself, but he still holds out a hand in case I need it.

"I'm glad you're here," I tell him.

"I know," he says once I'm situated on dry land.

"No, I mean, I'm glad you're *here*. I'm glad you're my stepdad."

"I know that, too." He smiles.

We roast marshmallows on the beach. I keep an eye on the sun as it inches toward the water. Time's almost up.

When it is more dark than light and we have to squint to see each other outside the circle of fire, Mom and Mema and Hutch leave us to load the truck.

Coralee catches Bert reaching for my hand and gives an evil grin. She begins to hum "Leaving on a Jet Plane."

I throw sand at her and the flames sputter when it hits the fire. Then her words sink in and we all get quiet. Bert leaves for Brighton tomorrow. We look at each other. There are too many words and also not enough.

"So I guess this is as fine a place as any to say goodbye." I squeeze Bert's hand once and he squeezes back twice. I keep my eyes fixed on Coralee, because it is too hard to see the way the light dances across his face.

"I hate that word. Let's pick a new one," Coralee suggests. "How about jalapeño?"

"You want to say jalapeño instead of goodbye?" Bert turns toward her. "You can't just swap out words however you please."

Coralee crosses her arms. "Why not?"

"It would be chaos."

Coralee raises her arms like she is going to twirl. "That's me, Berto. The queen of chaos."

"Fine," I say before she can turn this into a whole dance routine. I know she's stalling. She doesn't want to say goodbye any more than we do. "Then I guess it's jalapeño for now."

Bert begins to stand.

"Wait." I tug him down again. "I—I'm not ready."

We have already talked this through endlessly. We've calculated the distance. Brighton Academy is approximately 780 miles from here. Eleven and a half hours by car. Bert will come home for Thanksgiving. Mom and Hutch promised to let me ride over with Mr. and Mrs. Akers for fall break. It's goodbye for now. Not forever. But still.

Bert and I both look to Coralee. "Okay, forget jalapeño," she says. "Huddle up, people."

We huddle and it turns into a hug that no one wants to let go. Hold on. Let go. Hold on. Let go. Grandpa taught me that life is a whole lot of holding on and then letting go until you can hold on again.

I don't think I can squeeze any tighter.

ACKNOWLEDGMENTS

This book is the third act in a story I never thought I would get to tell. *Roll with It* marked my debut as a middle-grade author and commemorated the people in my life whom I miss (love you, Mema and PawPaw) and the one who made me a mother (big kisses, my Charlie). It was also a love letter to small places with big hearts. If you've ever lived in a town like Eufaula, Oklahoma, you know what I mean.

Because of the students and educators who read and celebrated that first book, I was able to keep the good times rolling (pun intended) with *Time to Roll* and now *Rolling On*. It's due to those readers and to the infinite support of my forever editor, Reka Simonsen, and my agent and friend, Keely Boeving, that Ellie's story has continued. I never thought I'd be an author who could craft a sequel, much less a trilogy, but here we are! And even as it is coming to an end on the page, I know that Ellie and Coralee and Bert will continue to live on in my mind for the rest of my days. Don't ever let anyone tell you you're too old for imaginary friends.

All this to say, *thank you all* for the ride of a lifetime, and I hope Ellie and her friends and family keep a special place in your heart as they do in mine.